I0760693

THREE DAYS UNDER THE SUN

(AND OTHER TALES OF THE OLD WEST)

CHARLIE STEEL
Tale-Weaver Extraordinaire

THREE DAYS UNDER THE SUN

(AND OTHER TALES OF THE OLD WEST)

CHARLIE STEEL
Tale-Weaver Extraordinaire

CONDOR PUBLISHING, INC.
Lincoln, Michigan

THREE DAYS UNDER THE SUN
(AND OTHER TALES OF THE OLD WEST)

by Charlie Steel

August 2023

*Cover and Illustrations by Barabash Sviatoslav
(All illustrations property of Condor Publishing, Inc.)

Library of Congress Control Number: 2020937947

ISBN-13: 978-1-931079-60-0

Condor Publishing, Inc.
PO Box 39
123 S. Barlow Road
Lincoln, MI 48742
www.condorpublishinginc.com

Printed in the United States of America

These stories are dedicated to
all the brave men and women who,
looking for a better life, dared to go WEST.

TABLE OF CONTENTS

*1st printing, *SUNDOWN WESTERN TALES*, Sundown Press 2016

THREE DAYS UNDER THE SUN

We lay close to the ground, spread flat, breathing the dust of the baked earth and waiting for death. The ambush was sudden, and there was no time to circle. I understood the right and wrong of it as I looked out at the burning wagons, the horses, oxen, mules, and the human bodies that bristled with arrows that had sunk deep into bleeding flesh. This was Sioux land, we were the invaders, and they were fighting for their survival.

A horse screamed and thrashed; its four legs and hard hoofs beat the ground. Dust rose around it. A woman and a man, wounded and dying, called out for help, then fell silent. A baby, thrown in the brush, began to cry. There were no more than thirty of us lying prone against a ridge. I raised my head and looked up and down the line. I tried to see who would go to rescue the infant. No one showed signs of movement. All along the rise were grim faces and staring, frightened eyes.

A gunshot sounded, and a bullet whizzed over my head. I ducked back down. Most of us had rifles and pistols. Twice, the band of a hundred or more had attacked, and we had returned fire. Their number was lessened by a fourth. They had no need to risk more. By waiting, the sun would bake us. We would go mad with thirst and hunger, and they would pick us off one by one.

The baby continued to cry. The Sioux waited, and the infant's wailing increased. I couldn't stand the crying any longer. I crawled over and around the other survivors and continued along the hill. I held the Henry out in front and pushed forward on my belly. Dust rose up around me. I discovered a gully that quickly deepened. It was a welcomed surprise. I came close to the wailing baby and crawled up into thick grass and brush. The infant was there where it had fallen or was thrown, still swaddled in a blanket. Its little face was red with wailing, and when it saw me, it stopped. Still balancing the rifle on my forearms, I scooped up the tiny bundle and crawled backward with one arm.

A bullet clipped the brush beside me. I kept crawling, and there was another explosion. Lead burned my side. I stopped and rolled sideways. Leaving the baby in the grass, I took hold of my rifle with both hands. The firing came from a group of cottonwoods where I saw movement. There was another gunshot. An Indian was up the tree and standing on a branch. I took aim, fired, and the brave jerked backward and fell. I grabbed the baby and dove for the safety of the small arroyo.

The homesteaders must have seen me disappear into the ground, and they began crawling towards me and into the gully. The men came first, followed by a few women and several children. I counted twenty-eight of them. They started rushing down the arroyo, and I fell in line and followed. The rain-eroded trench deepened the further we traveled. Soon all of us were running in the arroyo that was thirty feet deep and ten feet wide. Anything was better than sitting exposed in the burning sun. Down here, there was shade on one side of the high bank.

As soon as the Indians discovered our escape, they would come at us, and we would be exposed from above. We continued on; the ground sloped further, and the arroyo deepened and widened. As we ran, it twisted and turned like an undulating snake. This would help hide us. We rounded a bend in the arroyo and splashed into a pool of water.

The twenty-eight thirsty settlers sprawled flat along the sandy bottom and scooped water into their mouths. I remained standing, rifle in one hand, the baby cradled in the other. Miraculously, the child had not made a sound since I picked it up.

I licked my cracked lips with my dry tongue and waited for someone to come to my assistance. I stood guard and observed the cliffs and the wash behind me, looking for movement. It would not be long, and we would be discovered.

When a dark-haired woman finished drinking and stood up, I thrust the child into her arms.

"Here," I said. "Don't let it cry."

I ran further along the wash and found another standing pool of water. I knelt down and drank. The cool liquid burned my parched throat, and it hurt to swallow. I took in as much as I could and then moved back to a group of men and whispered.

"Watch the rear! Five of you climb up and guard the ridge. Don't expose yourself! We can't stay here. I'll scout ahead and look for a better position."

Without taking time to see if my directions were being followed, I turned and ran down the wash. I discovered a tributary to the right, and I took that. It widened, and I found more water. Further on, there grew brush and a cluster of trees. Before the trees was an intermittent stream. I ran back up the arroyo and signaled for the group to follow. The sound of distant gunshots came from above and then closer return fire.

"Send someone up to get those men!" I yelled. "The rest of you come along!"

I ran forward, and the remainder followed. We raced up the other wash into the wide-open area. We took shelter behind large cottonwoods. There was a natural barrier of logs near the water, thrown there by previous floods. I pointed and gave orders. The men grabbed other logs and added them to the pile. Soon we had a makeshift fort of dry peeled timber.

Gunfire continued. Several men from the wagon train appeared. They jumped and skidded down steep banks, holding rifles as they descended. Several fell, rolled, regained their feet, and came running towards me as I gave signal. Up on the bank, running Indians appeared; I aimed at one, fired and missed. From behind me came a fusillade. Several Indians went down at once.

The men made it to our log fort and dove for cover. I did the same as a band of Sioux on horseback came galloping along the far crest. They began to shoot down on us. Behind the cover of logs, we returned fire, and a number of mounted Indians were struck and fell. The attack ceased.

I sat back on my haunches and looked around. The baby began to cry, and someone called out for it to stop. A grim smile came to my face. For the first time, there was hope. We had cover, water to drink, and shade from the hot sun under the trees. Still, we could be surrounded and fired down upon. We needed to improve our log barricade.

I stood up and gave directions for more logs to be gathered. Men jumped to the task. Our barricade was built into a square with four sides. Within a short time, we had four solid walls of logs to hide behind. The fourth wall extended over the water. In this manner, we could drink without exposing ourselves to Sioux arrows and gunfire.

Within a short time, we saw glimpses of Indians work their way along the cliff above us. Two settlers were fired upon and wounded while gathering logs. We returned fire, and the men were rescued. We took crowded refuge in our wooden fort. Then there was silence. All we heard was the gentle rustle of leaves high up in the cottonwood trees.

The remainder of the afternoon, we rested in the shade, and all of us took turns sipping the cool water of the low basin. We had our lives but very little else. I had a rifle, pistol, and the cartridges in my belt, but the others were nearly out of ammunition. We had no horses, food, canteens, or blankets. Two of the men were wounded, one seriously. I had no idea of our chances for survival. But, I knew for certain that if the baby had not cried and I had not chased after it, we never would have found this refuge. We were a hundred times better off in our new barricade.

The sun gradually sank lower in the sky. Given water, the baby quieted and went to sleep. Men's voices rumbled and complained. I was no part of that.

I was a trapper turned explorer and found myself needing money, so I signed onto the wagon train. They hired me as a scout, third in command. My main job was to be a lookout and provide fresh meat. Before the attack, I had little contact with these settlers. I am now the only experienced Westerner left alive. I had no idea how we would get through this. We were the invaders, this was Sioux land, and we were smack in the middle of their territory. All they had to do was surround us and wait. We would weaken, and soon our ammunition would be gone. What was I to do with this group of greenhorns?

Out of habit, I stroked my Cherokee grandmother's necklace that I wore beneath my buckskin shirt. She gave it to me when I was a child.

"Remember your people," she said. "Wear this always, and it will protect you from danger and give you long life."

From that day on, I had never taken it off, and I was still alive.

In the dark, I could easily slip out by myself and escape. I thought about it and gave up the notion. It wouldn't sit right with me to just let these homesteaders be. Still, the thought of long, slow torture over a roasting fire…well, I had seen that too. It was up to me. I had to think of something, and soon.

Before sundown, there was sporadic fire and then dark. The Sioux, a religious folk, feared death in the dark. That was a blessing for this group, but I still posted rotating guards. In the morning, we had water for breakfast, tightened our belts, and waited. It was a pretty and fairly cool spot. If death were to come, it was a good place to die. That is if it was quick. I ordered the men to save a bullet for the women and themselves. Then we waited.

Time wore at the nerves of the greenhorns. The men talked, and the women stared stony-eyed. I had to break up more than one fight between the men. One was loud and verbal, the other a fistfight. The woman holding and caring for the baby was older, like myself. She had black hair and honey-colored skin. Her teeth flashed white when she spoke to me. Despite my age, I had no experience with women.

"Señor Stone," she said. "The baby needs milk, or she will die."

I didn't know it was a girl. She was a tiny thing with white translucent skin and light blue eyes. There wasn't anything to say, so I didn't. All I did was shrug and point at the diminishing stream of water.

"My name is Rosa, Señor Stone. You need not be afraid to talk to me."

The dark-haired woman with flawless, smooth skin sat down on a small log beside me. Her beauty made me nervous. I turned my head away and stared out beyond the fort, looking for signs of movement. Her scent came into my nostrils, and it was a powerful thing. Never had I dulled my senses with tobacco, and her fragrance was pleasing. It disturbed and aroused a hunger in me that could not be ignored. Yet I tried.

The baby whimpered weakly. The woman had a wet rag which the child sucked on. She held the infant towards me so that I could get a good look.

"No other man risked his life for this child. Señor Stone, you are very brave. I came to you so that you could see the baby and me. If we are to die, I want to do this beside you."

I still didn't know what to say.

"I got lucky, Rosa," I said. "We all got lucky when I found the gully and the arroyo."

"It is not luck. It is bravery that saved the child, and it is your bravery that found the water and the protection of this place."

"It was luck, Rosa, and a little bit of knowledge of the country."

"Have you lived out here long, Señor Stone?"

"Call me Stoney," I said. "Everyone else does. I came west when I was young—before the forty-niners. Stayed ever since."

"Do you know these Indians?"

"Yes. They're Sioux, and we're on their land. Should have known they'd be hopping mad about us crossing over. Each year more wagon trains come, and they want it stopped."

"Do you live near?"

"You mean here? No. I had a place in Colorado, up in the mountains. But it got lonesome. Last year I hooked up with a wagon train to California. I built a little cabin on some land above Frisco. I needed money for cattle, so I came back to St. Louis, and that's how I hired on as scout for this here wagon train."

"Will we all die?" asked Rosa suddenly in her soft accent.

I turned my head and stared at her, and she looked back with deep dark eyes. Eyes that a man could get lost in. She scooted close to me on the log, and her leg touched mine. I could feel the heat of it. My face began to burn.

"It doesn't look good," I murmured.

Her staring eyes embarrassed me. I turned to gaze over the low basin, and then up to the cliffs above. I thought I saw movement, and then I was sure. Indians were filing along the edge of the cliff.

"Look out, boys!" I shouted. "They're trying something. Look sharp!"

Men gathered along the wooden logs and peered through cracks to where I pointed. They shoved the barrels of their rifles forward and waited. A group of Indians tried sliding down an animal trail, hiding behind low rocks and clumps of brush. Dust rose; I raised my rifle and fired at exposed flesh. The Sioux I hit jumped up and then fell over. A marksman in our bunch aimed and fired carefully, saving on ammunition. Two more braves were hit. Others tried to drag them back up the cliff, and we fired in earnest, killing two more before the rest retreated. It appeared to me, we were in a very good defensive position. The warriors could not come at us from the cliff. To get down in the basin from any other direction and near the trees and log fort, required exposure. There was no more movement, and quiet returned.

"That's saving ammunition," I praised the men. "Only fire if you have a clear shot."

I went back and settled on the log where Rosa sat. She held the baby naturally in her arms, humming something soothing and low.

"You are a good leader," Rosa whispered and went back to rocking and humming.

"Only because there is no one else," I told her.

"No, because you are a man."

Again she came close, and I felt the warmth of her leg. Startled, I moved back. She laughed softly and scooted close yet again.

"You are brave with men," said Rosa. "But, I don't think so much with a woman."

"I never have spoken with a woman alone…." I started to say and stopped.

"Never?" she asked.

She looked straight up into my face, and the whites around her dark eyes widened in an expression of surprise and mirth.

"I, I never had no chance," I stammered.

"Then, Señor Stone, I give you the chance. Today, tomorrow, we may die. You sit. You talk to me. We get to know each other before it is too late."

Again I stared at this beautiful woman. She stared back, and there was a smile on her lips and in her eyes.

"I, well, ma'am…I just don't know what to say."

"Say what comes into your head, Stoney. I will listen, and we will enjoy our last hours talking together."

I felt my face burn, and it took courage to look at Rosa. The skin of her cheeks was soft and smooth, her lips naturally crimson. She, too, blushed, and a red flush rose along the top of her high cheekbones. In that moment, I could see all of her loveliness. Her dainty feet were small and well-shaped, and so were her legs. Her waist was narrow, and her chest was full and filled out the dusty-white peasant blouse she wore.

"You like the way Rosa looks?" she asked.

"Yes, ma'am," I managed to respond through a dry throat.

All that afternoon, while I watched carefully for further movement, she sat beside me, holding the baby. We talked of things I never imagined. She spoke words of hope and told me of her dreams of reaching California. I told her mine. Then she whispered other words, and to my surprise, I responded, talking of a possible future together. I described my ranch, high up in the mountains.

Another night passed, and Rosa slept close to me, the baby between us on the cool ground. Guards were posted, and I took early watch. In the morning, the birds came, and chirped their songs. Somewhere high up, it must have rained, for water began to run in the nearly empty stream bed. I heard movement above. It sounded like retreating hoofbeats of unshod horses. I thought that strange until the rumbling of wagon wheels came near. I climbed to the top of the cliff and peered over. A large wagon train was coming up the trail, and the Indians were gone.

***

There was condensed milk for the baby. A woman on the wagon train had twins, and she nursed the starving infant. The wagons camped above on the ridge and came down to water the livestock in the muddy stream. All thirty of us joined the train and spread ourselves among the nearly forty wagons. I was given a horse and went back to scouting and hunting for game. We passed through the Sioux nation and continued on up the trail to California. At night, I spent time with Rosa and the baby, and we talked.

"You saved the child; she is your responsibility," said Rosa. "She is as much yours as she is mine—she has no other family. Her name is Helen; I knew her parents. They were good people."

"I don't know, Rosa," I said.

I kept telling her I was too old to be a father.

"No," Rosa told me. "Not too old. Too scared. A brave man but in this thing not so."

Rosa talked to me every night, and every night I shied from admitting what I felt in my heart. *How could such a woman want a man like me?*

We struggled up over the high Sierras ahead of the snows and came down into California. We were going to pass close to my ranch. It was now or never, but I was too afraid to ask.

"I thought you were a man, Stoney!" said Rosa angrily on our last night.

"You'll meet a better man down in Frisco," I told her.

"You fool! It is you I want."

"All I have to offer you, Rosa, is a hard life of work and struggle."

"Stoney, we can make a good life together. I am not too old. We could have children. Good strong children that would work together beside their mama and papa."

When the wagon train rumbled out in the morning, I watched it descend the long mountain trail. It disappeared behind the pines. Standing beside me was Rosa, and in her arms, our baby, Helen.

LAMENTATION FOR BLACK KETTLE'S CHEYENNE

When he awoke, consciousness returned, and with it, memory and all the regrets of his life. He was swimming in grief—feelings so strong they were a weight too great for his body to bear, too heavy for his mind to endure. His soul ached for relief. He lamented his actions and his very existence.

What he had done, a Christian could never forgive. God would someday render judgment, and he and every man who had gone with Chivington would be condemned to everlasting fiery hell. William Bell wished for death to come and assuage the screaming images he carried in his head. Not in his sleep or in his waking moments had his mind given him relief. They had attacked Black Kettle's peaceful camp and brutally slaughtered men, women, and children.

It was what they did afterward that was the real horror that tortured him. His guts churned in revulsion. He could tell no living man what he had seen. He regretted with every fiber of his being joining Chivington's soldiers—no, not soldiers—renegades, murderers, scum of the earth.

William did not take part in the celebration in town. He was horrified by the reaction of the crowd and of the soldiers as they gleefully showed Indian body parts. The later article in the Denver Press glorified the tragic act of savage and violent genocide against the peaceful Cheyenne village. The truth did not matter. These white men hated Indians. It was Indian land they wanted, and to ensure possession without retaliation, the whites demanded death.

Taking a swig of whiskey from the bottle off his dresser and buckling on his gun belt, William resolved he would soothe his troubled conscience once and for all. Opening the door, he walked out into the hallway and followed it downstairs to the hotel saloon. There the revelers, still in mismatched uniforms, sat at tables or stood at the long bar, drinking hard liquor and boasting of their accomplishments.

Six of the most ruthless leaned against the bar. Several were still holding up body parts and bragging how they would turn the skin into tobacco pouches. William clenched his teeth in fury and shouted out.

"You cowards aren't fit to live!"

Silence followed, and all eyes turned to Bell.

"You filthy bunch of killers!"

"Watch your mouth, Bell!" exclaimed one of the six.

"Indian lover!" shouted another.

"Face someone who can shoot back!" Bell responded.

The challenge became a physical presence that resonated throughout the saloon. Men rushed to get out of the line of fire, and the six stood alone in a tight knot facing Bell.

"Oh, go cry to your mama, squaw man."

"No, I have a higher authority in mind," replied William Bell.

The returning silence was broken by the quick scrape of a boot and multiple gasps. All eyes wavered between Bell's taut face and his right hand held over the grips of his revolver.

"Bell, you don't have to do this," said one of the six.

"Oh yes, I do," he answered in a voice strong and clear.

When the crashing sounds of gunshots stopped reverberating against the walls of the saloon, seven men lay bleeding and dying on the floor. William Bell's prone body was one of them.

ON THE EDGE

I hung to the edge of the cliff, the tips of my fingers clutching a ledge of solid granite rock. My arms stretched taut, and my feet dangled uselessly, finding no outcropping on the smooth stone. I tried to balance myself and looked down. It was a drop of more than six hundred feet. I whistled to my horse, and he whinnied above me. I looked up, and there he was looking down, his dangling reins too far away to reach. If I was going to get out of this predicament, I had to do it myself.

It was my own fault. Blacky, my mustang gelding, tried to warn me not to advance up the steep trail. He fought the reins. I got angry and spurred him. He reared up when the coiled rattlesnake struck at his legs. I went over the saddle, hit the trail on my back, and rolled off the edge of the cliff. On the way down, my feet hit a lip of rock, the soles slipped along with my body, and I managed to grab hold with my hands. They stung pretty bad, and there was torn skin.

Above me, my horse neighed. Good old Blacky. He would help if he could. If I was going to have a chance to get out of this, I'd better "do something, even if it's wrong." An expression my dad always used on me. Dear old dad, dead and gone now. He had sat in that rocking chair on the porch to his last dying breath, telling all those hair-raising stories. Not one of them came close to this one. What would he do?

I lifted a hand from the ledge and slapped it back down several inches to my right. My bodyweight pulled when I did. I nearly lost hold. I needed to slide my hands along the wall and continue until I found some outcropping that would allow me to climb with both feet and hands. But the rock below me was as smooth as a baby's bottom.

Good thing my son's not here. He always likes to ride ahead of me. His foolish pony might have jumped off the cliff to avoid the snake. Then how could I live with myself? Still, this is a mighty foolish situation for a grown man to find himself in. I've got to get back up that cliff. How will my wife and son run the ranch without me? They'd lose it, starve, or get run off. That three-hundred twenty-acre spread has a crick and spring. More than most ranches have in this dry Colorado country. Many a rancher would go after it, knowing I was gone.

I thought of my wife's sky-blue eyes and fine figure and my boy's mischievous freckled grin and corn-shock hair.

With renewed vigor, I pulled myself along with my fingertips. Again I nearly lost hold. If only I was wearing gloves. No, I needed to feel the rock with my bare skin; I might slide off with gloves on. My fingers were bleeding now, rubbed raw. Despite the pain, I slid my right hand and then my left along the cliff edge. I kept searching for a hold with my boots. Suddenly, my right toe caught on a lip of rock. I tested it cautiously and then added more weight. This gave me temporary relief from the strain on my fingers. I rested a moment and regained some strength. Taking a deep breath, I continued sliding to the right. This time it was easier, as I balanced my weight with the toe of my right boot.

I felt the sun move in the cloudless sky. It passed an outcropping of mountain rock and began shining directly down on me, a man who foolishly clung to a solid granite wall by his fingertips. Above, a buzzard drifted with extended dark wings. It caught hidden winds and sailed on past. I know because I saw its shadow and wasted precious energy looking up. It stared back, and I am sure it wondered.

Inching on, my toe hold was lost. Again I hung suspended by fingertips. Sweat poured from me, and my clothing was drenched. Worse, sweat poured into my eyes, and it stung. I would give anything to be able to pause and wipe them clear. Strength faltered, and my breath came in great gasps. I had no choice but to continue on lacerated fingers as I slid them along the rough rock. Again I found toe holds for both my boots. I rested. Another few moments and I surely would have lost my grip.

I thought of my wife, my son, and my ranch. Strangely, in my mind, I went over this week's work. It was a habit of mine to write down my weekly chores. I took pleasure in crossing out each item completed. It was my way of knowing I had accomplished something—that time spent was not wasted. It was what I was teaching my son. These idle thoughts filled my mind as I worked my way along the cliff. I must think of something, anything, to ease the strain and pain of holding on. I could not fall; I would not give up. My family needed me. "Please, God! Just help me out of this," I prayed.

I lost purchase with my feet again. My right hand slipped, and I hung there by my left. My toes, looking for a hold, found none. This time I would fall. In panic, I stretched my right foot further out along the wall. It touched a ledge! My whole foot came down and rested on it. I pushed up and grabbed with my right hand and then quickly with my left. I moved farther to the right, and both hands and feet now had solid holds and rested firmly on rock. I could rest now. Balancing against the rock wall, standing on my two feet, I let go with my hands. I wiped the sweat from my forehead and eyes with my shirt sleeve. Relief!

I balanced there, with my arms down by my side. Blood rushed back into them. My racing heart slowed, and my energy began to return. I looked up and saw Blacky with his head still hanging over the cliff.

"Hold on, Blacky!" I called with renewed confidence. "I'll climb up there in a moment."

My horse neighed. I looked to my right, and I saw a fissure some twenty feet away. It looked like it was a few inches wide and near the ledge I was standing on. From there, it went straight up the cliff. At the top, near the trail, it opened up. With renewed vigor, I placed my hands against the rock wall and slid my feet along the ledge. I balanced myself carefully and, in a few minutes, came to the crack.

I jammed a fist into the fissure above me and tried to pull my weight up. My hand held firm. I let myself back down on the ledge, rested a few minutes, and then started again. I placed a closed fist into the opening and pulled my body up while using the toes of my boots to push. I worked my way up slowly. With the exertion, the sweat returned, and my heart raced. I concentrated on what I was doing and did not look up or down. Several times a hand or a boot got stuck in the crack. I would get a good hold with the opposite hand or foot and work the other loose and continue up.

I was so busy concentrating on the climb that when I came to the ledge of the upper trail, I was surprised. With a final effort, I clawed my way up and over onto the five-foot trail. I rested flat on my back. It was an awesome relief. I caught my breath and could hardly believe I was alive. Then there was the soft muzzle of Blacky in my face. I laughed. Caressing his soft snout, I reached up for his bridle and pulled myself to my feet. I felt dizzy and totally drained.

"Well, boy," I said out loud. "With God's help, we made it!"

DEATH COMES LINGERING

If I'm going to die from that rattlesnake bite, I sure hope it comes quick. It bit me when I put my hand down to pick up a broken piece of cedar—a limb fallen from a huge dead, twisted old tree. I took my knife, cut a deep X, and then squeezed the blood out. Probably did no good, but I had to do something. For justice, I shot that rattlesnake. I skinned it and lay aside the meat to eat. I built a fire and set the frying pan to cooking. Then the poison began to take effect. I got the sweats, started shaking, and my arm swelled up.

I had seen other men who were bitten. I knew what would come next. My arm would blacken; the muscles would turn to mush. Even if I lived, I'd probably lose fingers, the hand, and part of the arm. Depended on how much poison went in. In defiance of my upset stomach, I picked up some of that rattlesnake meat and took a bite. I forced myself to chew and swallow. When I did, I smiled. It was no smile of pleasure. It was more a grimace of retribution. Like the Good Book said in Deuteronomy 8:15: “He led you through the vast and dreadful desert, that thirsty and waterless land, with venomous snakes and scorpions...”

That was the proper quote. When wandering through this Western desert, there were venomous snakes to strike the wayward, the wicked, the sinners like me. I was a man who could not get along with others. Even in childhood, I got in fights. Small and scrawny for my age, I usually got the worst of it. But, I never gave up, and even when I was losing, I made sure to get in my licks. I hurt them just as bad as they hurt me, sometimes even worse. They remembered and, after that, left me alone.

That was the kind of man I was. I was born that way. A loner, a boy child, and then a man who could not—would not—take orders from others. Back east, there weren’t many jobs a man could do by himself. So I came west and took up trapping, prospecting, and living on the deserts and mountains. The money I made I put away for some rainy day. I didn't need much. Yesterday I dug up a pocket of gold. Not a lot, but enough to sustain me a long time—perhaps with the savings I had—for the rest of my life.

Now I had to go and get snake bit. Just when my fortunes turned, and I could take it easy. Gold would be no good to a dead man. That pack on the mule would have to be taken down and hid. No use letting a stranger get it all. Besides, I needed water from the canteen.

I struggled to get up, and the sweat poured from me. I barely got the pack down and into some rocks. I took the canteen and lay down and swallowed water. My throat felt like it was beginning to close up.

My mind wandered to thoughts of the dead cedar tree. While alive, that cedar didn't grow much more than half an inch a year. Fine-grained, tough wood. I bet even with an ax or saw, dead and dried as it is now, a man would have trouble cutting the limbs. It took maybe five hundred years or more for that red cedar to grow that large, and it would take many years of hot sun and dry western air to make it fall. Even after death, it had its purpose. It held the soil, provided shelter for birds and animals, and now, while I lay dying, it shades me from the burning sun.

I became dizzy, the poison took control, and I...

***

"Marty! Have you been in another fight? Look at your clothes all torn up! Your nose! It's dripping blood!"

"I think it's broke, Mother."

"Whatever will we tell your father? The last thing he told you not to do was get in another fight at school!"

"There were five of them, Mother! They waited for me outside. You should have seen me! Two of them I got good, and I got my licks in on the other three!"

"For whatever reason, do you fight, Son?"

"Cause Ma, they tried to sass me! No one bosses me!"

"We'll see about that when your father gets home!"

***

I awoke, and the sun was burning hot. I squinted through slit eyes, and the sweat from my forehead poured down and into them. The salt stung fiercely, and I closed my eyelids. My mind was swirling in a confused rush of memories—things that had taken place years ago. Thoughts I had so long ago forgotten.

***

"Marty?" asked the smooth-skinned girl.

She was sitting on the back porch steps of the house. A giant oak tree grew nearby, and its huge limbs provided shade from the afternoon sun. Flowers were poking their heads up in the flower bed next to the house. The smell of dark soil, fresh green grass, and lilacs filled the spring air with their strong fragrances. I looked at the pretty girl, and she scooted closer. Her thighs touched mine, and the warmth passed through our clothing. She put her hands around my right forearm, held on tightly, and squeezed. I could feel her breath on my cheek, and it smelled like the peppermint candy we had just shared.

"Why, Marty?" asked the girl again. "Why must you go away?"

"Because. You know I don't fit in here."

"We've finished school. You can do anything you like. If I asked father, he could get you a job. We could be together."

"No," I said. "That's not for me."

"I don't want you to go, Marty. Your going west is just a stupid old dream. Stay, Marty, stay here, and be with me."

"I can't, Sue. I have to go...."

***

"I see you're all packed, Son."

"Yes, Father."

"You got the train tickets?"

"In my pocket."

"For a man going west, you sure are packing light."

"A western man has to pack and travel light."

"Son, you won't give up this foolish notion? You won't stay here in Pennsylvania?"

"No, Father."

"Then I wish you well. Write and tell us you made it safely when you get to St. Louis."

"I will."

"Write when you can, Marty. Tell us what the west is like...."

***

Hooves of humped-backed beasts pounded on the desert prairie. Thousands of animals stampeded, and the dark curly-haired beasts ran as one. The air pulsed with a deafening roar as I lay in the shelter of a deep hole along the creek bed while the ground shook. Buffalo were pushed by their own kind, and some stampeded from the steep cliff to the creek bed below me. Several animals fell, their necks and backs broken. They fought to rise, and blood trickled from huge black snouts.

It was a long time of pounding hooves and rising dust before the bison stopped running. I came out from the hole in the creek bed, the only place in the wide-open prairie that could have possibly saved me from being crushed to death by these many beasts. I climbed up on the back of one of the dead buffalo that had been pushed over the cliff and looked in all four directions. Densely packed bison shuffled along in a slow-moving gate. They were spreading out. Some of the spring grass was exposed. The humped beasts bent their great shaggy horned heads and began to tear at the green stems as they marched along.

Taking one of my many skinning knives, I cut at the dead buffalo. I peeled back the hide on one side and sliced off the hump, then slit open the throat of the beast and cut out the tongue—two of the great delicacies, and I would have both for supper. Wiping my knife, I went off in search of dried buffalo chips.

***

"You say you dug up this gold yerself! But Mister, we say you're a liar!"

"I be Mountain Martin!" I shouted. "I fought with bears, I've danced with buffalo, I've wrestled with Cheyenne, I climbed the shining mountains, and slept with catamounts! If you boys got the gumption to try to rob me, then have at it! Cause I'll shoot out yer eyes, slit your bellies, and chew on your guts!"

The three gold thieves rushed me. I aimed one-handed with the Hawkins and plugged the largest in the belly. It drove the thief back and to the ground to groan and moan out his dying breath. The second man fired his rifle, and the round passed through my shoulder. Pulling my belly pistol, I shot him through the right eye. The third man raised his rifle to shoot, and my long-handled blade sunk deep into the would-be thief's throat.

***

"Chief Lone Wolf asks Martin to stay."

"Can't, Chief," I said. "I've got mountains to climb, rivers to cross, a shining sea to see."

"He, who walks alone, is brave. Someday, you come back to the People."

"Chief, the Cheyenne have taken me in and made me blood brother. I will hold the memories. Someday I will return."

"Good. My people will dance and sing, and we will feast."

***

Snow swirled, and the wind blew. The fire burned in the hearth, and most of its heat was lost up the chimney. I sat next to the flames and leaned in, trying to absorb the warmth. In a blackened pot, a fragrant stew boiled. I held a heavy buffalo blanket around my shoulders, the fur turned inward.

When will this winter end?

The cabin creaked with the force of the wind. The hoarfrost from the cold coated everything except the items closest to the weak flames.

***

"Señor," said the Spanish officer. "You are in Californio! This is our land and forbidden for

Yankee adventurers! To the guardhouse with you until we decide what punishment."

A bullwhip cracked, and the lashing leather cut deep into my back. I winced with the burning, cutting pain of it. The cell they put me in was dirty with stale straw. Whoever had lain here before was ill. It smelled of vomit, feces, and urine. They gave me water and bread in the morning. For three weeks, I lived on such fare. Then they took me into a courtyard.

The sound of the cracking whip was a repeated reminder of the slashing pain. I collapsed and fainted long before the twenty lashes stopped. I came to and the pain burned in my back constantly without relief. A peasant woman applied grease to my wounds, and they took me back to my dirty cell. Days later, the Capitán ordered my cell door open.

"Americano! Let this be a lesson to your kind. Never again come to our land!"

I had come to see the ocean. Open and friendly to all I met. Never again would I be so foolish. Officials of all countries were alike, harsh and selfish with rules and meaningless orders to obey. I took one long last look at the sea and walked away into the hills. I did not go far before hiding in the brush and returning to the soldier's garrison that night.

As I rode away, I heard the Capitán shout in Spanish, "You fools! Follow him! Bring back the Gringo and my horse!"

***

I awoke, and it was dark. The air was cooler, but not me. I felt each pulsing beat of my heart in my right arm. I was groggy, delirious with pain and fever. Then I remembered the snakebite. The canteen was by my side, and I managed to get it to my fevered lips. I drank and collapsed into a mist of rambling thoughts.

***

The screaming Indians came in a running group. They ran quickly, scattered, and spread out, throwing spears and bending bows. Death flew whistling through the air, and some of the wooden shafts hit their intended targets. Several painted Cheyenne fell. A feathered arrow struck a rock next to me and shattered.

"Utes!" shouted Chief Lone Wolf. "Dirt grubbers and hide scrapers!"

"Maybe, Chief," I yelled. "But right now, they look like fightin' men to me!"

I aimed with my Hawkins, and in the distance,

a Ute warrior fell. Some of the screaming Utes reached Chief Lone Wolf. One attacked him with a knife and another with a war club. I stabbed the warrior who held the club but not before he struck Lone Wolf. The Ute with the knife thrust it towards my belly, and I jumped back. Taking my pistol, I aimed and fired, and the warrior grasped at his chest and fell.

I bent down and lifted Lone Wolf over my shoulder. More screaming Utes ran towards us. Balancing the Cheyenne on my back, I began to run in the opposite direction. Blood from his scalp dripped heavily on the ground. Other Cheyenne came to protect their Chief, and some stayed behind to meet and fight the attacking Utes.

***

"The furs you have brought us are the best tanned hides I have ever purchased," said the German merchant. "I hope you will bring more next year."

"My Cheyenne friends did these," I told him. "Those are mine."

"Here is the money. Nearly six hundred dollars."

"Not enough," I complained. "Not nearly enough, but I'll take it."

"Martin," said the merchant. "My daughter has asked for you. She invites you to dinner tonight. She will be most displeased at me if you refuse."

"As her father, I am sure you have objections?"

"Nein, not at all. If you were to become part of the family, I think our business dealings would be much stronger. I have many silver trade goods. The kind the Indians seem to have interest in. If you were my son-in-law, I vould…."

"Thanks, but no thanks. I'm a free man, and I intend to stay that way."

I left the hide warehouse and went to my horse. The dark little mustang bucked and kicked its rear hoofs twice in unison before settling down. A pretty fair-haired female stepped out onto the shop porch. She was wearing a peasant dress, revealing a strong, healthy young woman.

"Vater!" yelled the young lady in anger. "Vhere ist he going?"

"I am afraid, away from us!" said the disappointed merchant.

***

The wagons came across the prairie in a long caravan. I watched their white and gray covers shimmer under the sun's bright light.

The Plains Indians will not be happy with this, I thought.

Ever since the gold strike in Colorado, nearly forty thousand have invaded the territory. I heard they also discovered silver. The country's changing. The whites shoot the buffalo, take the hides, and leave the carcasses to rot in the sun. The Cheyenne, the Sioux, Arapaho, Utes, Kiowa, Comanche are all up in arms. It's not even safe for me to travel.

I heard gunshots. No, not attacking Indians. Those greenhorns were shooting at buffalo for sport. I squinted and watched. A number of rifles all along the wagon train went off. I shook my head. They didn't stop to take a hide, a tongue, or even the hump.

***

The sun rose and lifted its shining array to a dark horizon two more times. On the third day, I lay in a flaming delirium. Through the fever, intermittently, I had lucid moments. I thought I heard voices.

"Who is he?" someone asked.

"That there's Mountain Martin!" said a familiar voice. "Haven't seen 'em since fifty-seven. Thought some Injun lifted his scalp."

I squinted and saw a buckskinned scout and youngster.

“Looks like snakebite!” he said, and I felt him go to his knees. “Why, he’s burning up with fever! Boy, you ride for the wagons and tell that doctor man ‘bout this.”

“Yes, Jim,” said the young man.

He mounted and rode away.

I could just make out the scout going to his horse and getting his canteen. He returned and poured water over my sunburned face, trying to get me to drink. Some went down, and some was coughed up. He continued until I swallowed.

“Martin!” he began. “Wake up, you old cuss!”

I opened my fevered lids and jerked my head up.

“Who is it?” I asked.

“Marty,” said the man. “It’s me, Marty. Jim Bridger!”

I tried to focus.

“Here, have some more water!”

I drank, and then with the old man’s help, I sat up.

“Jim,” I said, squinting my sunburned lids. “Where’d you come from?”

“I’m taking a passel of greenhorns through here. Pays good, even if the company’s not.”

“Jim, I got snake bit.”

“I see that, Marty. You’re all swolled up. Afraid that other arm won’t be no use.”

“I think I met my match this time, Jim.”

“I reckon, if you say so. Got anyone to leave a message for?”

“No. Sure good to set eyes on you.”

“Same here, hoss.”

“Jim, behind that rock is my pack. It’s got my life savings and some raw gold. Set you up good, it will.”

“Awww, Marty. Surely you got some kin somewhere, an old sweetheart, someone….”

“No. I’m glad it was you…come up…on me.”

“Marty, old feller, you sure had the times. I recall that Chief Lone Wolf telling me how you saved….”

“Jim!” I whispered and fell back. “I can see….”

***

I saw clouds and a shining white mountain. I was walking a ridge and held that old Hawkins in my right hand. It was cooler up there in the Wet Mountains, and I could gaze out far as the eyes could see. Miles and miles and miles of land shimmered down below; I reveled in the sight and wondered….

DOCTOR'S OFFICE

OLD MAN DYING

Doc Evans cared about four things in this life; sitting in the hot sun and warming his old bones, smoking a pipe stuffed with Gallaher Irish Tobacco, a good cup of hot coffee, and paying patients. In that order.

A rider approached on a dusty mustang. He was hunched over and swaying in the saddle. Doc Evans's keen eyes saw the drifter was badly hurt. He also noted the scarred saddle, the run-down boots, and ragged dress. Here was a broken-down cowboy with no money. Doc firmed his lips around his smoking pipe. Under no circumstances would he work a charity case.

The cowboy stopped his horse under the faded 'Doctor's Office' sign.

"You the doc?" asked the rider, holding the reins in one hand and his ragged coat closed with the other.

"That's what the sign says. What's the trouble?"

"A mountain cat jumped me back in the hills, tore me up pretty good. The claw marks are putrefying, and it hurts like Hades."

"Four bucks up front. If you need more doctoring, four bucks a day after that."

"Aren't you even going to look first?"

"Nope."

"What kind of doctor are you?"

"A poor one! Cause every broken down case in the county has paid me with promises, sacks of meal, chickens, and all kinds of paraphernalia. If folks I treated had given coin for my services, I'd be retired out of this broken-down town and living my ease up in Denver. Four bucks!"

The doc puffed furiously and with pent-up anger. A cloud of smoke rose around his head and nearly obscured the old man's wrinkled face.

"Mighty hard dealings," said the rider.

"Four bucks! No more charity cases!" fumed the doctor.

"All right. I got my lucky twenty-dollar gold piece. Carried it since the conflict. Saved my life at Chickamauga…stopped a bullet…."

"Don't need no hard-luck stories. Let me see it."

The rider reached in his shirt pocket and pulled something out. He held the object in his hand, looked at it briefly, and then tossed it to the man on the porch. Surprisingly, the doc caught the heavy coin deftly with one hand and examined it. On one side of the bullet-pierced coin was stamped Clark Grubner & CO. 1860, and on the other side, barely legible, read Pikes Peak Gold, Denver.

"You fought at Chickamauga?" asked the doc.

"I did."

"What side?"

"Does it matter?" asked the rider gruffly.

"Suppose not. I was there. Treated men from both sides."

"Bet you made a pile of limbs…."

The doctor rose angrily to his feet.

"Sonny! I been accused of that all through and after the conflict! I never did nothing but what had to be done—with what I had to work with! If'n you want to be taken care of, don't insult the only medicine man in these parts!"

When the doc stopped shouting, he commenced to cough…he bent over in a fit of agony, and his wracking cough, deep down in his chest, revealed that he was very sick. It was some time before he recovered and stood up. A handkerchief held to his mouth revealed specks of blood. The young man on the horse saw it.

"All right, Doc," said the rider softly, now swaying weakly in the saddle. "As you say."

"This gold piece is damaged!" shouted the doc. "Give you fifteen dollars credit!"

"You're a hard man…" began the rider, and then he slumped sideways.

The cowboy caught hold of the pommel and weakly slid off the saddle and onto his feet. Then he fainted dead away and dropped to the ground. A barefooted kid, skipping down the street, ran over to look at the prone man.

"Well, don't just stand there!" growled the doc at the boy. "Harvey, you git yourself up to the Sheriff's office and bring him and that deputy back. Tell them I'm too old to be hauling drifters and hard cases."

The boy named Harvey grimaced at the mean-mouthed doc and ran up the street.

***

"You're a fraud, Doc," said the injured man lying on the cot. "You've got a soft spot in you a mile wide."

“Shhhhhhhh! Tarnation, man! Don’t let anyone hear you!”

“How long have I been lying here?”

“Seven days, eight, if you count this morning,” answered the doctor.

“You said four dollars a day. I figure I’m five days past that fifteen dollars I paid you. And that Indian cook of yours has been bringing me meals since I woke up. How much do I owe you for that? How come you didn’t throw me out?”

“That mountain lion tore you up pretty good,” said the doc. “I sewed over a hundred stitches in your back! And you were all infected and clean out of your head with fever. I couldn’t throw a sick man on the street.”

“You could have, but you didn’t.”

“Just say I got a soft spot for any soldier who fought at Chickamauga.”

“If you say so. But as soon as I am able, I’ll get a job and pay you back every penny I owe.”

“You better, Son. And you can start by telling me your proper name.”

“It’s Fisher, Doc. Daniel D. Fisher.”

“Well, Danny, soon as you’re up to it, I’ll send you over to Pepe Lopez.”

“Who’s he?”

"He's my Mexican partner. He and I own a pig farm. We supply all the pork and ham this town can eat. I earn more off that place than I ever did doctoring. Seems people will pay up front for food."

"You want me to work for this Lopez?"

"Well, you don't have a job, do you? And you owe me money! Don't tell me you're too proud to slop hogs!"

"Well, Doc, a man does have his limits."

"Tarnation fellow! There's a drought on, the grass is sparse, and the cattle are dying. There's not a job to be had in fifty miles! If you're serious about paying me back, you'll work for Lopez!"

"Like I said before, you're a hard man."

***

"Well, Pepe?" said the Doc. "Tell me all about it."

"Señor, this young man you send me, he all the time work. He never sit still."

"Good. Tell me what he's done."

"He drive me crazy, all the time fixing things—the fences, the pig pens, the cabin roof. When the pigs are fed, he look for other work and cuts and chops the firewood and then looks for more to cut. He works on the well and the irrigation ditches. All the time talks about plowing more land and planting and irrigating more corn."

"Well?"

"He ask me questions and talk, talk, talk."

"What does he talk about, Pepe?"

"Sometimes he asks about you. Questions I can no answer. He ask about our little ranch, how many pigs we raise and sell each year. He asks me about the well and the dry creek bed and how much water runs in the spring. Sometimes he ask me the same questions---who owns the land beyond the ranch and how much an acre costs."

"What do you think of him, Pepe?" asked the doc.

"I think for a cowboy, he knows a lot about farming and pigs."

"Is that a bad thing?"

"Sí Señor. Before he come, I sleep in the morning, take my siesta during the day, go to bed at night and sleep in peace. This young man come, this Danny, all he do is work, work, work, and ask the questions. I think if he no go soon, then I go crazy."

"All right, Pepe. When you go home, send him to me."

"You promise he not come back? Before he come, Pepe happy, now he come, Pepe tired…want things like before. We shake hands Señor Doc, this Danny, he not part of promise…."

"All right, Pepe. I'll see to it that he won't bother you anymore."

The doc shook Pepe's proffered hand, and Pepe Lopez smiled in relief. Then the old man bent over in one of his coughing fits and did not stop for a long time. When Doctor Evans recovered and wiped the blood from his mouth, his Mexican partner was gone.

***

"You wanted to see me?" asked Danny Fisher.

"Yes," answered the doc.

"What's it about? You're not happy with my work?"

"No, just the opposite,"

The doctor attempted a smile, making his wrinkly old face turn up in a surprising expression of warmth.

"Pepe told me you more than paid me back."

"Then what is it?" asked the cowboy.

"Pepe can't stand the pressure of all the work you're doing; he wants you off the place."

Danny Fisher looked up at the doc in shocked and disappointed surprise.

"He wants me off the place? Because I work…?"

"Calm down, Son," said the older man, who actually laughed. "You know, people surprise me all the time. Now, when I first saw you, I thought you were a no-account drifter, not worth…."

A dignified older Indian woman in a plain print dress came onto the porch with a tray and two cups of coffee. Next to the coffee were plates with large slices of cake. The two men sitting on the porch thanked her, and she disappeared back into the doctor's quarters.

"Take Rosita there," said the doc. "She's genuine one hundred percent Cheyenne. Showed up at my door onc day, looking for food and work. I had my doubts but took her in. You know, she's the best darn cook I ever had. She can boil a good cup of coffee, and she's the one who cured those infections. Turns out she knows a heap about Indian medicines and remedies. She brewed up several plants, and that's what we applied to your back. Since she came to work for me, I haven't lost a patient."

"You say Pepe Lopez wants me off his place because I work too hard?"

The doctor laughed and slapped his knee. Then he picked up a fork, took a bite of cake and a sip of coffee. After a long pause, he answered the young man.

"Don't pay attention to Pepe. A man like him gets set in his ways, and he doesn't like change. Especially on his own place."

"What will I do now?" asked Danny in a dejected tone of voice. "I don't have a red cent to my name."

"Why don't you start by telling me more about yourself. You haven't told me much."

"Well, Doc, there's some things a man don't…."

"Why don't you tell me about how you came to fight in the war."

"I was young and foolish, full of all the wrong notions. I thought it would be a grand adventure…."

"Didn't turn out that way, did it?"

"No…"

"There isn't a morning…a day…a night… that the images of that war don't come into my head," said the doctor.

"I know," replied the young man. "The nights and the dreams are the worst. Can't shut the images off then."

"That war was an awful thing," said the doc in

a low stern voice. "It killed and wounded a lot of men, tore the nation apart…scarred a generation."

"Yes, it did."

"Well, Danny!" said the doctor, suddenly changing the subject. "Eat your cake and drink your coffee! I want to talk to you about something, but before I do, tell me about your folks—where you came from."

There was a long silence, and neither man spoke. Several ranchers' wagons rattled up the main street of the small dusty town. The rising sun began to throw light on the porch, and the old doc seemed to turn his body to it and welcome the extreme heat.

"Doc, I don't want to talk about it."

"As bad as all that? Pepe tells me you know a lot about farming and that you've been around pigs before."

"If you must know," sighed Danny.

"Yes?"

"My old man, he owned a farm back east, ran mostly milk cows. If you know anything about that—up in the morning and work to dark, attend to the pigs, the chickens, the cows. Done that ever since I was a little kid. Regular as clockwork, and I came to hate it."

"Yes?" said the doc. "Go on."

"I grew up shoveling manure, milking cows, slopping hogs, doing farm work. When the war came, I talked of joining. My old man was hard to deal with. He wouldn't have none of it. Told me it would be a sin to take up a gun and kill my fellow man. I was young, didn't see it that way. We argued, I left, and he told me to never come back. So after the war, I drifted…."

"And that's how you know about farming?"

"Yes."

"And once you got started at Pepe's," said the doc. "You discovered you liked the work—that you were good at it."

"Yes! How did you know?"

"By the way Pepe described your work. He told me you asked who owned the land next to his place."

"Yes, I did. I thought maybe…."

"That you could work that land, maybe put up a dam, sink several wells, plant more corn, raise more hogs."

"Why, yes!" said Danny. "Not just hogs but a few steers. And hosses. I always wanted to raise horses. I thought about breeding Morgans with Mustangs and get a better riding mount…."

The doc held a cup of coffee in his hand. His wrinkled face was smiling, and it actually made his sour expression completely disappear. Danny Fisher looked at the old man in wonder.

"Well!" said the doc. "Sounds like you got ideas and a good head on your shoulders. How about if you and I become partners? I just happen to own that land, far as the eye can see, clear to that ridge of mountains back yonder."

"But Doc," said Danny with surprised wonder in his voice. "It would take money to...."

"You supply the plans and work, and I'll supply the funds."

Again, there was a long silence. Quietly and efficiently, Rosita returned with a fresh pot of coffee and this time with a tray of cookies. When she took up the two forks and empty plates, Danny saw her smile and wink at him.

"Well!" shouted the doc. "Don't just sit there with your mouth open! Tell me what you think!"

"Doc, how could you trust a drifter like me? Why would..."

"Pshaw! Hasn't Pepe Lopez given me a good report? Didn't Rosita and I doctor you when you had the fever? Didn't we hear you go on about your Ma and Pa and your kinfolk back in O-hi-o? Can't an old man know when he's met a good, decent, hard-working young fellow?"

"I don't know what to say. It's more than I ever dreamed...."

"Say yes!" called Rosita from inside the house.

"You see!" said Doc. "Even Rosita agrees."

"All right," replied Danny Fisher, putting out his hand. "You got yourself a deal."

The old man smiled, and his homely wrinkled face again changed into a pleasant visage. The two men shook hands. Then, quite suddenly, the oldster began to cough. Out came the white handkerchief, and afterward, there was blood on it. Danny stared in stony silence.

"Kid, it's no surprise to anyone. I got the cancer."

"How long...?"

"It's been coming on for quite a while. Who knows about these things? I got maybe a month, maybe six; that'd be my professional opinion."

"I see," said Danny. "And what about our agreement?"

"Well? What about it?"

"After, who would get your half?"

"I don't have a living relative. You just take Rosita and have her work for you. Will you promise me that?"

"I will. Is there anything else?"

"Now that you mention it," replied the doctor. "There's a Saturday night dance coming up. You missed the other ones working out at Pepe's place. Now there's a young lady I'd like you to meet. She runs a little dress shop in town. Twenty years ago, I brought her into this world myself. Her names Margaret but everybody calls her Peggy…."

"Doc!"

"Well? What's wrong? Can't an old man look after people he cares about? Before it's too late? Oh, and by the way, here's your lucky coin back."

The old man pulled the pierced gold coin from his pocket and handed it to Danny.

"Doc, you're not at all what you pretend to be."

"Careful boy! Watch what you say, or you'll git me all riled!"

From inside the doctor's quarters came the warm laugh of Rosita. On the opposite side of the street, a pretty young woman in a smart dress and hat stepped out of the mercantile. She was carrying a basket of food items.

"In case you're interested," said the doc in a teasing tone of voice. "That's Peggy!"

BODO'S GENERAL STORE

FIGHTING FOR PARADISE

Bodo Rolke objected to anyone calling him a foreigner or mentioning his strong accent. If asked, he invariably had a vitriolic response.

"I am American! Don't nevermind anything else!"

Bodo came from some small eastern European country that spoke a Slavic language. What country and what language it was, Bodo Rolke refused to say. Nor would he explain how he left Europe and came to America. If asked, he would growl and yell and protest the very need for explanation.

"I come vest for freedom! To be American! Just like you!"

The town of Paradise was exclusively his creation, and he named it. In a lush, green, hanging valley at 7500 feet, he began with a general store, a saloon, and then a hotel. It grew between the mountain climbs of Colorado, not far from Badito, and the more distant Pueblo. It was very near the Taos Trail over the Sangre de Cristo Pass to Fort Garland.

As Paradise remained small, Bodo became the self-appointed mayor and town marshal. Eventually, he sold the saloon and hotel for profit and governed the town from the porch of his general store—a cup of coffee in one hand and a double-barreled shotgun in the other.

"Voman," he complained to his New York-born wife. "Vhy can't I teach this tongue of mine to speak plain American? I'd cut it out myself if I didn't need it so…."

"Never mind," replied Mrs. Rolke. "Once people get to know you, they overlook your little accent. You have done great things here. I don't know if Paradise will become an important city, but it won't be for lack of trying."

"True, voman, what you say," replied Bodo, thumping the butt of his shotgun on the wooden planks. "I didn't fight Indians, renegades, and thieves to lose. Paradise vill grow bigger than Denver. You just vatch!"

Out onto the porch came a dark-skinned young woman with long gleaming raven hair that fell to her waist. She was dressed in a simple frock that accentuated her willowy frame. Three small children ran beside her—a girl with long blonde hair and two boys, one with red hair and the other with dark curls covering his head in a circling mass. Here were three children of vastly different features and a young maiden who clearly contained Indian blood. Mrs. Rolke, very religious and unable to have children of her own, did not believe in cutting the hair of her adopted brood. Her favorite story in the Bible was Samson, and it was her great pride to leave the locks of her youngsters alone.

"Father," said the older girl. "We are out of airtights and running low on tobacco, coffee, and other items. Here I have written a list."

"Thank you, Alice," replied Bodo, setting down the shotgun and taking up the paper.

"Children!" said Mrs. Rolke stepping onto the porch. "Leave your sister alone and come to the kitchen. Help me set the table for supper."

The youngsters disappeared into the store. Far in the back lay the kitchen and rooms for the Rolke family.

"Daughter," said Bodo. "I'll give this to that Jim Stone. I expect the freighter to pass through here tomorrow. I have a load of elk and deer skins for him to take back. I'm proud of you, girl. You finished this list just in time."

The young woman smiled and disappeared through the door. Bodo shook his head in wonder at the way his eldest could slip away without making noise, perhaps a gift from her ancestry. He took up his coffee cup and drank down the last of the tepid brew. Foot on his now prone shotgun, the middle-aged man leaned back in his chair and looked over his domain. It was his favorite pastime, and he could observe Main Street and each passerby from his perch.

Paradise was far enough from Badito and Pueblo that the surrounding miners, ranchers, and lumbermen came to the small town for supplies and entertainment. Some of those who traveled to the area and liked the town purchased plots and built homes to become community residents. Mayor Rolke made the land available at a cheap price in an effort to expand growth. Having no stagecoach system, the mayor arranged to have the young freighter, Jim Stone, haul passengers to and from his village. They used the freight wagon to reach Greenhorn Station to catch a stagecoach south to Trinidad or north to Pueblo and eventually Denver.

One late afternoon, Bodo, sitting on his porch, relaxed and fell into a light sleep. It was his own loud snore that woke him. Before him stood the most bedraggled wretch he had ever seen. The man wore a combination of patched and dirty clothing, worn moccasins, and around his shoulders a ragged blanket. The fellow's face and hands were horribly dirty, and his hair was long and unkempt. From the distance of the porch and the twenty-some feet to the bottom of the steps where the man stood, Bodo could smell the odor emanating from the poor fellow and see pieces of sticks and leaves in the man's hair.

"Can I help you?" asked Bodo after some very uncomfortable seconds of examination.

"Me hungry," said the wretch.

Bodo's speculation was confirmed. This human was some kind of outcast Indian, of that he was certain. The poor fellow did indeed look like he was starving.

"Sit there at the steps, and I vill have food brought to you," said Bodo. "Emma!"

The wife came running.

"You bellowed?" said the panting woman opening the screen door. "What on earth is…."

Emma Rolke stopped and stared at the strange man sitting on the steps.

"Voman," said the store owner. "Can't you see this poor fellow is starving? Hurry! Fetch some food."

The startled wife disappeared, and within minutes their daughter Alice came, tray in hand. A bowl with vegetables and meat stew, a thick slice of bread, a steaming cup of coffee, and a spoon was on it. Without hesitation, the daughter gave the tray to her father. He, in turn, descended the steps and handed the bedraggled man the offering. The stranger's face wrinkled into some attempt at a smile. Still seated, he took the tray and placed it on his knees.

"You good people," croaked the fellow and then picked up the spoon and began to shovel food into his mouth.

"Alice," said Bodo. "Thank you for being so prompt. You can go now."

The girl did as she was told and quietly disappeared. Bodo returned to his large chair and sat. It wasn't long, and the Indian finished eating.

"Good food! Thank you."

"I've never let a man go hungry, and I never

vill," said the mayor. "Now, suppose you tell me your name."

"In my life, I have many. You call me…."

The name that came from the man's lips was unpronounceable and made no sense to Bodo.

"I can't say that," the store owner replied. "Suppose you give me something simple?"

"Then call me Chief," said the scarecrow of a man.

"Alright, Chief," said Bodo taking the tray from the Indian and setting it on a chair. "My name is Bodo. Velcome to Paradise."

"Par-a-dise?"

"Yes, the name of this town. Now tell me, is there some vork you are looking for?"

"No one gives me work."

"I vill," replied Bodo. "Suppose you tell me vhat you can do?"

"I hunt good. Shoot deer, elk, rabbits."

"Yes? Anything else?"

"Nothing more," said the Indian.

"I have use for hides and for meat, but mostly I need someone to cut vood. Vinter's coming, and I need all the vood I can get. Vould you be villing to chop and cut vood?"

"Woman's work," replied the Indian.

"No, in our vorld it is a man's vork. For cutting vood, I vould give you pay."

"What pay?"

"A cabin to live in with a varm stove. Money, twenty dollars a month. New clothes to vear and soap to keep yourself clean."

"What I cut wood with?"

"I'll furnish a cart and a mule to haul the vood, sharp axes, and a saw. You cut and saw the pieces into two-foot lengths and pile them against the lean-to along the store. If you vork hard, I vill pay you those things."

"How long?"

"As long as you are villing to stay and cut vood."

"Days free?"

"Yes, Sundays."

"I work," said the Indian, and then he attempted another of those gruesome smiles and put out a hand to shake.

Bodo had no choice, and the nearer he got to the man, the stronger the odor. The two men shook hands. Despite his wasted appearance, the Indian's grasp contained great strength.

"Come in the store," said Bodo. "I vill have my

vife help pick out clothes for you to vear. There's a bathhouse in back, and we'll fix you hot vater."

"You good man," repeated the stranger.

"Chief, I need a vood cutter. You do good vork; you stay as long as you vant."

While boiling water on the kitchen stove for the bath, Mrs. Rolke questioned her husband.

"Why did you hire that scary fellow?"

"Every man deserves a chance," replied Bodo.

"He looks like he would cut our throats in our sleep."

"Judge not, lest you be judged," replied the head of the household.

"Sometimes, husband, I think you go too far."

***

Jim Stone drove his large freight wagon and four horses in front of the general store. The freighter set the brake and jumped off. A passenger, holding a sack of supplies, climbed down and went up the street. On the front porch sat Bodo Rolke, shotgun in hand.

"Hello, Pops," said Jim. "Don't you ever go anywhere without that gun?"

"I am the town marshal as vell as the mayor. I

vill keep the peace here, and any robber needs to know that."

"From what I heard, you haven't had a robbery in years."

"This shotgun and my vigilance is the reason vhy. Vhen I first came here, I had to fight…."

"I've heard the stories before, Pops. Where is that lovely daughter of yours?"

"I have told you before, Jim, my name is Mayor Rolke, or even Bodo, but never this Pops. Please stop the disrespect. Here is the list of supplies prepared by my daughter—a young lady you vill never be permitted to go near. There are the bales of elk and deer hides. Take them and go."

"Someday, Pops, someone will get near that pretty girl of yours, and there will be nothing you can do..."

"It von't be you, Jim," replied Bodo.

In anger, the older man rose from his chair, walked to the end of the porch, and picked up the first heavy bundle. In a quick swinging move, he turned and, with both hands, threw the hides through the air. The heavy weight flew across the expanse and landed in the wagon bed with a loud thud. Bending once more, Bodo lifted the second bundle of elk hides, weighing well over two hundred pounds, and threw that in the wagon. The heavy landing was loud enough to make people on the street stop to look where the noise came from.

"All right, all right, Mayor," said Jim. "I get it. Perhaps some of those stories you told me were true. I'll be back in a week with the supplies, Sir."

"That's better," responded Bodo, and this time he smiled at Jim.

The freight driver took the supply list and climbed back up on his wagon seat. Two male passengers from the town had taken the opportunity to climb aboard; they rested their shoulders against the large hide bales. Both men headed for Greenhorn station to catch the stagecoach. Removing the brake, Jim slapped reins.

"Until next time, Mayor," shouted Jim.

Bodo waved and sat back down, once again picking up his shotgun.

A crunching noise came from the woods on a trail next to the store. It was Chief, leading a large cart full of wood. Bodo left his shotgun, climbed down the porch steps, and greeted the Indian.

"It looks like a good load, Chief," said Bodo. "Let me help you."

Together they carried two-foot sections of logs to the lean-to and stacked them.

"At this rate, ve'll have enough to get us through most of the vinter."

"You help me keep axes and saw sharp," said Chief, "and I'll keep you in wood."

The Indian was greatly changed from when Bodo had first met the man. He no longer looked like a scarecrow. He wore a plaid wool shirt, canvass pants, and jacket; a wide belt and knife were around his middle. Hidden in one of his boots was a smaller knife and sheath.

"How you getting along in your cabin?"

The Indian attempted that smile.

"Stove keeps me warm. Better, Alice brings me good supper."

"That vas Ma's idea. She told me you do good vork. She favored that haunch of venison you brought her. Asked special if you vould like to come to Sunday services."

"What you call church? God and Jesus?"

"Yes, that's it. Ve set up a few benches in the store. It starts at ten; after, ve eat."

"I will come," replied Chief.

"Good. If you need to know the time, I can send...."

"No bother, the sun tells me. Now I take mule and cut more wood."

***

In a week, Jim returned with a wagon load of supplies. This time there were two paying passengers on the front seat and three in the back. The passengers climbed down. Bodo called for help to unload the wagon. That included Mrs. Rolke, Alice, and the three young children. Jim worked hard and didn't say much as he carried heavier items into the store. When the wagon was unloaded, the freighter handed over the invoice, and it matched the supply list. Bodo paid the bill and watched the young man place coin into a money belt.

"Your suggestion to carry passengers worked out for me, Mr. Rolke. I am gaining a tidy profit from riders. More than what I thought possible. I want to thank you for that."

"It vasn't hard to see the need and solution, young man," said Bodo. "But appreciate the sentiment."

"I didn't tell you that the stage line, Barlow and Sanderson, wants to hire me as stagecoach driver. I turned 'em down. There's better money hauling freight and passengers on my own."

"Folks like clever and reliable young men,"

said Bodo. "Owning your own business is a better choice."

Sir," said Jim. "I wonder if I could talk to you privately."

"Yes? Step outside, and you say vhat's on your mind."

"Sir, I have been very disrespectful to you."

"Yes, you have," replied the store owner.

"I misjudged you," said Jim. "I thought you were a phony, but I found out those things you said…."

"You have been talking to others about me?"

"Yes, Sir, I found out that…."

"You find out I have substance, and now you are polite? I think a fellow of real character vould be polite first and then find out vhich is the correct trail to follow."

"Yes, Mr. Rolke, you're right. I have been very immature in my behavior."

"Vhat do you vant from me, Jim?"

"I would like permission, Sir, to speak with your daughter, Alice."

"And vhat vould you say to her?"

"Why…I…I would ask if she has interest in me and if I could…."

"Court her?"

"Yes, that's it."

"You do vell to ask me first. And your change in behavior comes as a surprise to me. Go finish delivering supplies, and I vill think about this. You vill have my answer next time ve meet."

"Thank you, Sir."

"Go on, be off vith you," said the father.

Jim went down the steps of the large porch, hesitated, turned around, and climbed back up. He approached the older man.

"Sir, I don't think you take me seriously. I want to...."

"All right then, you like my daughter, tell me vhy."

"Because...she...it's difficult to put into words. I..."

"If you can't do better than that, Jim Stone, vhy should I consider letting a rude man like you come anyvhere near my daughter?"

"Because, Sir, each time I see her, she takes my breath away. When I'm near her, I feel different. She's always so calm, so quiet, so peaceful. When she is close, a warmth envelopes me, and I want to reach out and touch her...."

"Pushy, but better," said the father. "Go on."

"When we unloaded the wagon today, when I was handing things down, our hands touched. It made me feel…so…so different. Like I want to protect her. It's always like that when I am around her. Ever since I first saw her, talked to her, I've done nothing but think of Alice. Awake, asleep, she is always on my mind."

"You have spoken to her?"

"Yes, every chance I had. Every time I've come here."

"And she speaks to you?"

"Not in the beginning, but when we were alone in the store, I would say things to her. It was easy to see she was shy, but I kept at it. At first, she only smiled. Eventually, she began to respond, and although it was only small talk, I could tell she liked me. If I was given permission to see her, Sir, I am sure…."

"Vhat are your intentions?"

"Why, marriage, of course," said Jim adamantly. "That is if she would have me."

"Her heritage is different than yours. She's…"

"A very smart and beautiful woman, Sir."

There was a long silence.

"I'm glad you came back to explain yourself,"

said Bodo. "Now go on, be off vith you, and let me think about this."

Jim smiled and then ran down the steps and climbed up on the wagon. Bodo Rolke watched the young man drive away, and to his own astonishment, he caught himself smiling.

"Alice!" shouted Bodo.

The screen door spring twanged and gave away Alice's presence.

"You heard?"

There was no reply.

"Don't be coy vith me, daughter. Ever since you vere a little thing, I've known that you have ears like a fox. There is very little that you miss. I'm villing to bet you vere on the other side of that door and heard vhat vas said."

"I did hear a word or two," responded Alice.

"Good. That makes it easier. Vell?"

"What, father?"

"Vell? Is vhat he said the truth of it? You have interest in this young man?"

The golden complexion on Alice's face darkened.

"This is one time being silent vorks against you, Alice."

"Yes, father. I like him, and I want to see him."

"He did say marriage. Alice, you're eighteen years old and…."

"I have liked him since that first day, Father."

"Then it's settled," responded Bodo. "You have my permission to step out with young Jim Stone."

Alice ran into her father's arms. He held his daughter and hugged her back.

***

Paradise did not expand but seemed to remain stable. Ranchers came in for supplies on weekends, and passing travelers stayed at the small hotel. Having time on Sunday, miners came to the saloon, and many ate at the town restaurant. All these folks visited and purchased items at Bodo's General Store and paid respect to the man in the chair with the shotgun—a tough man with a funny accent and a peculiar name.

The Indian they knew by the name of Chief continued to cut firewood, and the stacked pile under the lean-to eventually filled up. There would now be enough wood to last through the winter and far into the spring.

Chief worked steadily and, with his great strength, had replenished the firewood in half the time of prior woodcutters. Besides working for Bodo, the Indian was paid for cutting and stacking wood for the saloon and hotel. That was in addition to the meat and occasional tanned hides the older man provided. Chief was the best worker Bodo had ever hired. The Indian lived quietly and said little. The merchant hoped he would stay a very long time.

There was one issue that concerned Bodo. He had witnessed the Indian observing Alice with unusual concentration on several occasions. The store owner worried about it. Someday soon, for the protection of his daughter, he would have to ask Chief the reason.

***

Jim Stone continued to earn more money by hauling passengers on his freight route. Each time he came to town, he extended his stay long enough to spend time with Alice. Alice smiled and talked more, and a pretty young woman before, she became radiant in the presence of her betrothed. It looked very much like the Rolke family would have a new son-in-law before Christmas.

***

There had always been tough and dangerous men living in the mountains. There were still renegades, thieves, outlaws, and occasionally Indians who escaped the reservation and caused havoc. Not without good reason, protesting the theft of their land and their lost freedom. Lately, a group of outlaws was working the trails between Badito and Fort Garland, jumping riders on the way to Taos and rustling cattle. With the advice of Bodo, Jim began carrying a Henry rifle and a Colt revolver. It was not for decoration that Bodo had the shotgun. The young man practiced shooting with Bodo behind the grocery store when visiting Paradise.

"It vill be many years before this country is tamed," Bodo told Jim and his family, "if ever."

The following Saturday, Jim arrived at midday and delivered goods early so he could visit with Alice. They were out back, sitting in the family picnic area. Bodo briefly observed the young couple. *I hope,* he thought, *they tie the knot soon.* He worried about Jim risking his life traveling through the mountains by himself. Bodo was sure Alice could convince the young man to quit freighting. He and Emma weren't getting any younger, and it was time to let the younger couple help run the store.

The sound of iron wheels crunching over rock came from the trail near the store. It was Chief with the cart and another heavy load of firewood. The old Indian raised a hand in salute to Bodo and passed by. Bodo remained at his perch, shotgun at his feet. Today was not particularly busy. This was a warm fall afternoon, and the temperature was nearly perfect. A slight breeze blew, stirring pine limbs and rustling the mayor's hair. *It's good to be alive,* thought Bodo. He felt content sitting in his chair and overlooking the town.

Then he saw them. He knew instantly that trouble was coming. Bad trouble. Eight men on spirited horses rode past the store and towards the saloon. Such horse flesh was a rarity to be seen at any time in these mountains, and eight of them at once indicated who these men were. The horses were dark, as were the dress of the eight men. The riders were bearded, wearing wide sombreros, and heavily armed. Some wore two pistols, and on each mount were saddle holsters with more revolvers and scabbards containing rifles attached to each saddle. These were outlaws, gunmen, killers. Of this, Bodo Rolke was certain.

The town marshal rose from his perch, and doing his best to hide his shotgun from view, he bent down and picked it up. Taking one last look, he watched the men dismount and tie up their horses in front of the saloon. He could hear raucous discourse and crude comments. For the first time in his life, he doubted if he could keep his family and the town of Paradise from harm.

As Bodo rushed through the store to the back kitchen, two thoughts entered his head. The mayor wondered what reaction the outlaws would have had if they saw him holding his shotgun—or if he had been displaying the marshal's badge Emma had been so pushy about him wearing. Surely they would have shot him down. Then what good could he have done for his family?

"Emma," whispered Bodo, finding his wife busy preparing supper. "Stop and listen to me. Eight men rode in. They're killers. Take the children and go down in the cellar. If they burn the place, use the cave in the voods. Hide there until they're gone."

"What about Alice and Jim?" asked his wife.

"I'll send Alice down. I need Jim to help me protect the store."

"Do you think they'll come?"

"They're at the saloon now. They'll need supplies and ammunition, and I'm sure after a few drinks, they'll be here. If they behave themselves, I'll let them go."

"Eight is too many, Bodo. Even for you."

"No time to discuss it. Go!"

Their young children were helping set the table when Emma called them. "Listen carefully, and don't say a word," the woman said firmly. "We must go to the cellar—now!"

Bodo stayed long enough to see Emma light a lantern, open the cellar door, and herd the children down the steps. Then he went outside and hurried to the backyard. Jim caught sight of Alice's father and instantly came to his feet. The older man had observed the two sitting on a peeled log, his daughter in Jim's arms. The young man had just kissed her.

"Sir!"

"There's trouble," said Bodo. "Jim, I need your help. Alice, no time to explain. Run to the cellar and join your Ma and the children. Hurry!"

Alice opened her mouth to say something and her father, for the first time in his life, yelled at her.

"Do as I say, Alice! Don't you dare question me on this!"

Angrily, the young woman turned and ran towards the back steps.

"What is it, Sir?" asked Jim.

"Take up your guns, Jim. There are eight outlaws in town, and I guarantee you there's going to be trouble. Come vith me, and ve'll set something up inside the store."

Bodo and Jim raced through the kitchen and entered the general store. They encountered Emma emptying a box of .12 gauge brass buckshot shells.

"Vhat are you doing, voman?"

"Don't question me, husband. It'll take three of us, and that's still not enough."

"Chief is out there, but it vould be too conspicuous to get him," said Bodo. "He misses nothing that goes on. I hope if things get rough, he'll help."

"Me too," said Jim. "What do you want me to do?"

"Take this box of .44-40's and go stand behind the far end of the counter," said Bodo. "There's a pile of saddles and blankets there, and they won't see you. Any men on your side of the store are yours to cover with the rifle."

"If they start shooting?" asked Jim.

"Don't miss," replied Emma Rolke.

Bodo took down several bolts of cloth and two shotguns. The double barrels he loaded and placed on the counter and then set cloth bolts over each one. The store owner pointed, and Emma stood behind the counter, the disguised weapons before her. The husband handed Emma several rounds of shotgun shells that she placed in deep pockets of her apron. She was a stout woman, and the big pockets hid the heavy ammunition. Bodo took down another shotgun and loaded it, along with the one he always carried. He placed them on the counter and put a blanket over them. He set a box of shotgun shells on the lower shelf.

"Now, what do we do?" asked Emma.

"Ve Vait," replied Bodo.

Time passed.

"Voman," said Bodo. "Vould you get us some sarsaparillas?"

"You want one," replied Emma, "fetch it yourself. I'm tired, and it's been a long day."

Bodo Rolke laughed, went to the kitchen, and came back with a stool for his wife. Then he went to a storage room and returned with three brown, pop-top bottles. He handed one to Jim and then to Emma.

"Here, voman," said Bodo. "Sit down and take the veight off. Have a drink, quench your thirst."

Emma Rolke eyed her husband, sat down heavily, and sighed.

More time passed, and the three waited. From across the street, they heard loud laughter and then shouts. This was followed by several gunshots.

"Maybe they'll be easier to handle with drink in them," said Jim.

"I doubt it," replied Bodo. "From vhat I saw, these are killers. Probably soldiered in the Great Conflict. If they start something, don't hesitate to shoot because they von't."

"Don't miss, Jim," said Emma. "I promised Alice I'd look out for you."

"I did, too," said Bodo.

Emma turned to look at her husband.

"When did…"

The screen door hinges screeched and the long spring twanged. Several men entered the store, each of them talking at once.

"Well…looky here!" said one of the outlaws.

"You men take up some of these sacks and start filling it with supplies," said another.

"Yes sir, Captain," came a response from a third outlaw.

Bodo took a keen look at the man they called the captain. It was obvious he was their leader. There was a saber scar along one cheek of the man, and he wore a right holster Colt. Under a faded confederate shell jacket was a shoulder holster. Bodo counted five men. Three came to the counter. Each man was unbathed and saddle-weary. They wreaked of horse and human sweat.

"We want all the .44-40 shells and .38's you have," demanded the leader. It wasn't a request; it was a command. "We'll also be needin' some percussion caps, powder, and lead. Hurry up, old man! We don't have all day!"

"Yes, sir," replied Bodo, and he took a quick look at his wife and began searching for the items the man requested.

"Is this your place?" asked the captain.

"Yes, it is," responded Bodo.

"Heard a bit about you. They say you started this town.

"True, I did."

"They say you've set yourself up as town mayor and marshal."

"More an honorary thing than real," replied Bodo in self-deprecating tones.

"Sounds like a good racket to me," said the captain.

"Ve make a living," said Bodo.

"I'm afraid you're going to need a new restaurant owner," said the leader.

"Vhy is that?" asked Bodo, stopping in his tracks and holding onto boxes of Henry rifle ammunition.

"Before one of my men shot him, he felt obliged to tell us that you also do a little banking. Says you have a safe back there behind that wall. Suppose when you finish with the ammunition, you open it and give us all your money."

The other outlaws laughed. Bodo came up to the counter and dumped the ammunition boxes on it. Then he looked eye to eye with the leader of the outlaws.

"I vill do it," said Bodo, "if you promise not to hurt...."

"I'll promise nothing, you foreigner!" shouted the leader, pulling his army conversion Colt and pointing it at Emma. "But what I will do is shoot your wife...."

All the time the captain was talking, Emma had worked her right hand under the bolt of cloth, and it was now wrapped around the grip of the shotgun and her finger on one of the double triggers. Before placing the shotguns down, Bodo had pulled back the hammers of all four. As the pistol came up to

Emma's head, Bodo shoved both hands under the blanket in front of him. His fingers touched the triggers. He squeezed, and two shotgun barrels emptied into the bellies of the leader and another outlaw standing beside him. Both men were blown back in a gory mess.

"You von't shoot my wife, and I'm no foreigner! I am American!" shouted Bodo.

As hardened as they were to violence, the other three outlaws were shocked by the sudden explosions and the splattering blood. Surprised by their leader's death, they were slow to pull their pistols. In another second, Emma fired her other shotgun, and it struck the third outlaw near the counter in the chest. The man fell, and airtights scattered across the floor.

The two killers near the door, pistols in hand, aimed to shoot. From the other side of the room, Jim Stone fired his Henry at one of the two outlaws left standing and missed. Simultaneously, Emma, Bodo, and Jim each fired another round. Two shotgun blasts and one rifle bullet found their targets, and the last two robbers fell.

Bodo bent and grabbed a handful of shells. Still holding his shotgun, he vaulted over the counter and ran for the front door.

"Jim!" shouted Bodo. "There's three more of them out front! Hurry and cover me!"

As Bodo shouted, pistol shots blasted from in front of the store. The merchant slammed the screen door open and raised his shotgun. One barrel still loaded, he caught sight of an outlaw with a smoking pistol in hand. Bodo aimed and fired. The buckshot hit the killer's head. Dead, he fell backward.

Bodo quickly opened the shotgun, jammed in two shells, and slammed the barrels back in place. Jim had come up behind, his pistol at the ready. But there were no more outlaws left alive.

From the height of the porch, Bodo and Jim could see the last two outlaws lying face down in the street. Knife handles protruded from their backs. At the bottom of the steps lay the Indian, Chief. The old fellow moved his head and slid one hand over a gaping wound.

"Jim," said the town marshal. "Vatch for trouble!"

Bodo ran down the steps and knelt over the woodcutter.

"Chief!" said Bodo.

"I got two, but third man, he got me," said the Indian.

"You did real good," said Bodo in earnest.

"I speak to my dead wife's sister," said Chief. "She tell me she came to Par-a-dise and give my young daughter to you. This, before soldiers imprison my people. I finally escape reservation. I come to take her with me. But now I see she have better life here."

"I knew there vas something…" exclaimed Bodo.

"Never tell her," said Chief. "Tell no one. Help her have…."

The Indian fell back, and the sun clearly showed the wrinkled dark features etched into the face of the man. A bullet hole in the chest of the brave fellow was welling volumes of blood. It flowed across a flowered shirt, black vest, and dripped to the ground. Abruptly, eyes opened, and the Chief spoke once more.

"You good man…take good care of daughter..."

The long sigh of escaping breath was clearly heard by Bodo. Then came the sound of footsteps climbing down the porch.

"Boy," said Jim. "I always knew there was more to the Chief than what he told us. This proves it, he sure saved our bacon."

Bodo Rolke looked up at the young man and smiled faintly.

"That he did, Jim. That he did."

A RUNNING GUNMAN MAKES A DECISION

His canteen was empty, and below lay a squatter's cabin. If he was to continue running from the posse, he and the mustang needed water. The farm was built in a depression on the undulating prairie. In front of the house was a well. The place had a rundown look about it. It was a dry prairie farm, and the torn earth near it was cracked and contained desiccated remains of failed plants.

There were a hundred such places across the Colorado grasslands, and most looked exactly like this one. No matter how much work a family put into the hardscrabble farm, they would never do better than survive. If they made a living, it was not from the crops. More likely, they shot and lived off antelope, mule deer, the large hares, or the few remaining buffalo. If they had money left, they purchased supplies, and if they didn't, they found work. La Junta was not far off, and it was a growing community.

Swifty rode down the hill and towards the house. Coming nearer, he could see part of it was a dugout; its front and sides were built of adobe bricks. Brush and dried clay covered the exposed roof. The rear, cut into the hill, made for an unknown-sized interior. Good thing it didn't rain much. The sun-dried adobe would soften under a steady downpour, turn to mush, and cave in.

Dried clothes were hanging on a line running from the well to the awning of a crude porch. A faded blue dress fluttered in the wind, along with a man's shirt, a boy's pants, and a little girl's dress. Various other clothes had fallen and were lying on the bare hard-packed earth. Nearing the home, only the horse's hoofs made an echoing sound. There was an ominous silence about the place. Something was wrong. Swifty felt it. The horse smelled the air, snorted, and backed nervously from the porch.

The man got down off the tired mount and tied the reins securely to the porch post. There was a water trough near the well, but it was dry. It would turn out to be a good thing.

"Hello, the house!" shouted Swifty.

There was no answer except the sudden gust of hot prairie wind and the rustling of clothes from the line. The thirsty outlaw pounded and rattled on a half-open door. No answer. Cautiously he peered in. The stranger pushed the door wide open, and sunlight illuminated the form of a man lying on rough wooden planks. On the vast open room floor lay what looked like a human figure. Even in daylight, it was difficult to see into the darkened interior.

Against his better judgment, Swifty entered the cabin and bent over the man. A dry wheezing sound came from the prone figure. Shaking the farmer brought no response. A harder shake and a digging of stiff fingers into the man's overalls caused the farmer to open his eyes.

"What's wrong with you, feller?"

"Fever," whispered the homesteader. "Sick—all of us."

The man closed his eyes and went back to struggled breathing.

"How many are there?" Swifty asked

No matter how he poked or shook the man, he did not open his eyes or respond.

Swifty looked around the cabin. It required lighting a candle. By moving towards the blackness of the back wall, he discovered a large open interior with no barriers. The farmer was a poor builder. By not having windows, the place was little more than a cave. It was unnecessarily dark and oppressive. One window would have made a huge difference; two would have made it livable.

In the back, against the left wall, was a blanket barrier. Behind it stood a small bed in which lay a child. It was a little girl, and she also was breathing heavily. The outlaw gasped. The child's blonde curls and pale skin reminded him of his younger sister. The stranger felt her forehead, and it was burning with fever. He left the child and explored further. More blanket barriers were found, another bed, in it a sick boy, perhaps ten or so. Against the far wall was a larger arrangement of rope and blankets, and behind was an adult bed where lay a sick woman. She smelled badly of soiled bedclothes. Vomit crusted her nightgown, bedding, and floor.

Swifty held the candle before him and quickly exited the dark adobe interior. In the bright sunshine and fresh air, he took a deep, cleansing breath. Here was sickness, and it looked bad. These four were near death. The father must have been the last to be stricken. He was the only one fully clothed and not lying in a bed.

This was serious. It could be typhoid, cholera, or some other disease that came suddenly without warning and killed all that were exposed. Swifty had touched the little girl, the poor thing. Would he now get what they had? Swifty looked up the hill and out onto the vast stretch of the open sky. If the posse found his tracks, they would be upon him within a few hours. He must get water and move on. Yet now, that did not seem like such a good idea. He must boil the water first before it could be drunk. That much he learned from attending the very ill in the drafty tent encampments during the Great Conflict.

I am a fool to think of staying. Best to get on the mustang and ride hard and fast away from this sickness. Surely, these folks are beyond hope and are all going to die.

The vision of the pretty little girl lying on her bed against the dirt wall of the dugout had burned an image into the mind of the gunfighter. The woman, the man, and the boy he could leave, but never the little girl. It would be like leaving his little sister.

Against his own arguing mind, the man went to his horse, loosened the cinch, pulled the saddle off, and slung it over a partially broken and half-finished railing. He did the same with the damp horse blanket. The horse remained tied to the post by reins, but the bit was pulled from his mouth.

Swifty looked at the blazing sun in the pale sky and then all around him in a circle, taking in the large open distances of the prairie and the slope of the front hills. There was no sign of the posse. He breathed in the fresh, clean air. Death was no stranger to him, and if he was going to die, the way of sickness would be his last choice. A swift bullet, a thrusting knife, or a fall from a rolling horse was the form of death he thought would come to him, but never a slow-moving illness.

The outlaw took another large breath. Then, he laid down his sombrero, rolled up his shirt sleeves, and set to work. The lone man kept up a steady pace without tiring. He thought logically and set about what he must do. The first thing he did was tear up the wooden planks of the inside flooring. He hauled enough of these rough-cut boards outside to cover the dirt under the awning in front of the dugout. Next, he carried out the little girl, the boy, the woman, and finally the man. He laid them down on the boards in the shade.

There was every reason to believe that the source of the disease was the water from the well. But, the family needed to be stripped, washed, kept cool, and given lots of water. The well was the only source.

Swifty found a large black kettle and two tin washtubs. He brought these outside. Dropping a bucket down the well, he drew up successive pails of water and filled the iron kettle. He searched for the farmer's supply of fuel. It was a combination of cottonwood and dried dung. Using these, he built a fire and began to boil water. Once boiled, he dumped it into one of the tin tubs. He kept this up until both tubs were filled.

It was an indelicate and miserable job to strip all four of their clothing. They were lying in and covered with their own filth, spewed forth from top and bottom. The clothing Swifty discarded to be buried or burned. He scrubbed the family using a rag, lye soap, and boiled water. When he finished, the flesh looked better, and the cool bath reduced some of their red color.

He gave them each boiled water to drink. It wasn't

long, and they spewed this up. Swifty repeated the process over and over, and each time he was forced to clean them. When he thought the water had given beneficial effect, he gathered the blankets from the interior and washed them in boiling water. When they were dry, he covered the family.

Swifty cleaned, scrubbed, boiled, watered, and administered carefully and efficiently; to the four sick patients. He tried not to think but performed each task with the necessity required. Occasionally, he did wonder what disease they had. Still, since he could do nothing about it, he worked diligently to give what comfort and care he could. The thought of the posse never left his mind, and often his eyes wavered to the hilltop, but only for a guilty moment before he returned to his work.

At first, he thought his efforts did no good. The little girl was closest to death, followed by the mother, the boy, and the father. The girl received the most solicitude from the caring man, and he did all he could think of. He found a cholla, filled it with water, and hung it high from the rafter. The water cooled in the wind, and he swiftly and liberally applied the cool wetness to the child's fevered skin. He did this over and over. Then he gave her water to drink, which she promptly threw up, and which he more promptly cleaned. This he did over and over and the same for the other three.

Expecting death any moment, somehow they lived through the night. In the morning, they appeared to be a little better. By the second day, all four were on their way to recovery. This gave Swifty time to go hunting. He shot a mule deer and brought it back. He boiled parts of it into a soup and fed each of them a spoonful at a time. He continued to care for them, and when the man was up and on his feet and the woman, boy, and little girl sitting up, the stranger collapsed from exhaustion. He lay at their feet, outside in the hard dirt, next to the wooden bed he had made for the four family members.

The homesteader and his family were worried. This stranger who had saved their lives seemed now to be struck with the illness and might die. The stranger himself lay under the blankets, on the boards, outside, and slept the clock around. When he awoke, he was ravishingly hungry. The family was immensely relieved.

"Don't drink the water!" blurted out Swifty when he awoke.

"But," said the father. "Isn't the water from the well what you were using?"

"I mean," said Swifty. "Don't EVER drink it unless it is thoroughly boiled."

"Why?"

"The illness came from the well," the stranger answered. "From now on, boil the water before using it for anything."

"Not for washing," said the man.

"Yes," said Swifty, "for everything. "I learned this from an army hospital."

"Nathan," said the wife. "Don't argue with the man who saved our lives. Stranger, what do we call you?" she continued, turning to the cowboy.

"My name's Swifty, ma'am.'

"Mister Swifty," replied the woman. "From now on, we'll boil every drop."

"Good, it's just Swifty, ma'am. I sure hope you didn't drink any water direct from the well."

"Nathan drew water," said the wife. "We haven't used it for anything except my lilacs which are planted on the side of the house. I hope they won't die. I brought them all the way from Shelby, Ohio."

"Mommy sure likes those flowers," said the little girl. "Don't you, mommy?"

"Yes, dear," answered her mother.

The little girl slid into her mother's arms, and she picked the child up and held her for a moment. The weakness from the illness was still upon the woman, and Swifty saw the unsteady movement.

"Are you all right, ma'am?" he asked.

"Why, Swifty. Don't you call me that again. To you, I'm Mary and don't you forget. You saved us, and you're part of this family—whether you like it or not."

"Especially after seeing all of us the way he's seen us!" laughed the father.

"Nathan Bently!" his wife corrected with great heat. "You just see what that crude remark gets you for the next two months! You just wait!"

"Aww, honey," said Nathan. "I didn't mean nothin' by it."

"Say," said the boy. "Did you really keep us all naked out here on these rough boards?"

It was quick for a woman still reeling weakly from her illness. The slap was hard and fast on the back of the boy, and it was followed by even a harder one to the back of his head.

"Aww, Ma, I didn't mean nothin' by it."

"You hush up, Bartholomew," said his mother.

"There will never be another crude reference. Is that clear? Mister Swifty saved our lives, and to him, we are eternally grateful. Now, hush up."

"Ma'am," said Swifty, his face turning red. "There's a haunch of venison left, and I am sure it will make a fine meal. If you think you all could eat whole food."

THE PROFESSOR GOES WEST

The driver kept cracking his whip with one hand while firing at the Indians with the other. The Utes on tired horses were beginning to slow. Reaching the final turn on two wheels, the stagecoach left its pursuers behind before taking the road into town.

"Aww," shouted down the driver. "Them redskins weren't half serious."

The stagecoach disgorged its passengers in front of the saloon and onto the main street. Dust stirred and swirled with each puff of wind and slowly settled. It covered everything in fine powder. The passengers patted their clothing and doffed their hats to beat the dust from their attire. Clouds of silt billowed off into the dry, thin air.

"What a country!" commented Professor Miller.

"Wind, dust, and heat! Extraordinary that people can live here."

The thin short man took out a large white handkerchief and attempted to wipe his spectacles clean. Squinting through them, he placed them back on his whiskered face. His light blue eyes were immediately magnified by the thick lenses. Amazed, the Professor looked off past the meager buildings of the town at the shimmering mountains. They rose in the distance, and white snow lay on the highest peaks. Below them, and in every direction, was the dark green of the forest. Below that, the beige and yellow prairie stretched out as far as the weak eyes of the Professor could see. The very vastness of the wide-open views shook the quiet reserve of the little man.

"Professor," said the driver. "The hotel's across the street. It's about as good as any in town. You'll find this here Trinidad the sure-to-goodness West."

"Driver," replied the Professor. "If this town is as lively as the steering of your coach, I am sure I will find it satisfactory."

There was a large crowd around the stage. Westerners come looking for any bit of entertainment and to see what the stage had brought. All were disappointed to see only a whiskey drummer, a seamstress with her two children, and the odd-looking man in a high collar and a rumpled suit.

The driver threw down the luggage in what the Professor thought was an excess of energy. The scholar looked for a man to carry his two valises. Finding none, he picked his bags out of the dust of the street and began to cross to the hotel. A buckboard with two horses passed swiftly before him, and then two galloping cowboys. The dust swirled up and settled heavily on the man with the luggage. His hands full, he had to blow the dirt away from his face with his mouth. It had little effect. Once at the boardwalk, he set the luggage down and took out the white kerchief. He wiped at his face and mixed with the sweat, the cloth came away beige brown. The little man grimaced, picked up his bags and went into the sudden shadow of the hotel lobby.

The lobby was small and airless. The clerk at the desk eyed the stranger with minor interest. The Professor set down his luggage and announced himself.

"I am Professor George Miller of Cambridge, Mass., and I would like one of your best rooms,

Sir. I will be staying indefinitely. I have come to research the West and will be here the entire summer. Perhaps your hotel has special rates for visitors who stay by the month?"

"Thirty a month," said the clerk.

"Why, Sir, that is exorbitant!"

"Eh?"

"That is far too expensive."

"Maybe so. Cash in advance for YOU."

"My good man, where is your superior?"

"There ain't none. I own this here place, and it's thirty a month, cash."

"If I am to pay such a sum, may I have my baths in my room?"

"Suit yourself. Every one of 'em comes with pitcher and basin."

The Professor eyed the man to see if he was serious. He was. Reluctantly the Easterner pulled out from a small purse a hundred dollar banknote.

"I ain't got change for that there thing," said the hotel owner.

The Professor stuffed the hundred back. He pulled out a change pouch and counted out a combination of gold and silver coins that summed up to thirty dollars.

"Now, if someone will carry up my bags."

"Mister, your arms ain't broken. You carried 'em in. You tote 'em up."

The little man gave the hotel owner behind the counter an indignant look.

"My key?"

"Number fifteen on the third floor. The door ain't locked."

Indignant, the Professor took hold of his heavy leather bags and began to climb the steep stairs. Outside, the Friday afternoon town was beginning to fill up. The thunder of hooves, creaking wagons, and loud voices filtered into the open door of the hotel. So did the resultant dust. The Easterner looked and saw layered clouds of the beige stuff drift under the bright rays of the hot sun. At the top of the stairs, the little man stopped to rest. Outside in the street, he heard galloping horses, accompanied by wild yells and loud gunshots.

The room contained one bed with squeaky springs, a scarred wooden chair, a dresser, a small mirror, and a pitcher and basin. There was no closet. The whiskered man sighed, put his bags on the floor, and went to the window. The street below looked magnified and distorted through the cheap leaded glass. Stifled by the heat, the little man struggled with the sill and finally managed to raise the bottom frame. The incoming air was no cooler than the inside. It blew gently, and furnace hot from off the town's main street.

The Professor grabbed the single chair and carried it to the outside view. He sat down, and again he sighed as he struggled to remove his heavy wool suit jacket. Succeeding, the man reached for his soiled handkerchief and wiped the sweat from his face. There he sat and looked out at the now bustling town. He wondered if his boast to research the West was perhaps a bit more of a bite than he could chew.

A few days before, he had stopped to see the coal mining camps outside Walsenburg. The experience was a distasteful scene he could not wipe from his memory. All those poor foreigners were huddled in a filthy slum of tents and shacks. The educated man saw for himself the blackened, weary faces of the men as they came from the mouths of the mines. The Professor knew who these people were and where they came from—men, women, and children, poor Europeans recruited off foreign streets by promises of good wages and good living conditions hired for America's coal camps.

He sat and thought about what he had experienced and about something he didn't even want to admit to himself. All the time he observed the coal camp, he was deathly afraid that the armed guards would make him a captive as well.

Professor Miller sat exasperated and numb with fear on the wooden chair and looked down on the town. How could he write the truth of what he saw and not be shunned and ridiculed by his colleagues? They would not believe what he witnessed. Worse, perhaps they would not care. He couldn't possibly write such an exposé; it would be too dangerous to do so—dangerous to his career and to his physical form. Should such a paper be written, he easily envisioned one or all of the rich industrialists sending a man to silence him.

Depressed and tired, the little man stripped and washed himself with a washcloth from the pitcher of water poured into the basin. Demoralized by the rough ride inside the stagecoach, he lay his sore body on the bed. He was really too pained and tired to sleep, and it was a long time before it came. He stared up at the ceiling and listened to the strange raucous weekend noises of the wild western town. His last thought before going to sleep was to question himself deep down inside his very soul. *Was he really man enough to confront and observe these westerners in their natural habitat? Was he capable of facing all the aspects of this raw West, or was he—what he was becoming to believe—a coward?*

After washing up and cleaning his teeth in the morning, he put on a boiled collar and shirt. He tied his tie and donned another heavy woolen suit. It was stifling in the heat. Tired of the stares and uncomfortable dress, the middle-aged man seriously considered purchasing western clothes. Downstairs he inquired from the owner about a good place to eat breakfast, and he was directed to the Alpine Café. Crossing the dusty street, he found it at the end of the block. It was a Spanish restaurant, and the menu was written in that language. He asked for ham and eggs, and coffee. He got what he ordered, but salsa was served with the food. The fare was cheap and good. It was the repeated stares by the patrons that made him decide to purchase new clothing.

The man at the general store smiled at the Easterner all the time he waited on him. The store owner talked him into trying on a complete outfit. The boots and hat took the longest to select. The simple canvass pants, shirts, vest, and bandannas were easy to pick out. He kept the rough garb on and had his suit folded into paper and wrapped. The western clothes and boots were much more comfortable.

Next, the owner talked him into a saddle and bridle. After all, if he was going to get around, he needed a pony. The man owned one of the liveries in town and promised to pick out a good "gentle" horse. Professor Miller had the distinct feeling he was getting in over his head.

"What about those Indians that chased us into town yesterday? Isn't it too dangerous to go riding alone?"

The dry goods man laughed.

"Don't you know those Indians are Utes? They've been peaceful for years. It's a joke between the stagecoach driver and a couple braves to fire a few shots. He signals when a greenhorn's aboard. It was a joke, Professor, for your benefit!"

Miller stared at the man and was completely lost for words. The entire incident seemed real enough to him. He would have sworn…

"What you going to purchase for protection?" asked the store owner.

"Protection?"

"Yeah. You know, from snakes, varmints, and the like."

"If I leave them alone, won't they let me be?" asked the Professor.

"Not necessarily. Now you take a mountain lion or a pack of coyotes. They'd as soon take a bite out of you as not."

"You're not serious."

"Never can tell when you'll need protection out here. Then there's the two-legged varmints. Never know when you'll meet up with a bad one."

"I'm afraid I'm not equipped to handle a situation like that. Besides, I don't see that you are armed, Sir."

The general store owner smiled broadly. His hand slipped into a pocket, and it came up with a derringer. Then he bent under the counter and produced a double-barreled shotgun. Putting that away, he stood up and pulled back his apron, exposing a holstered revolver.

"Out here in the West, a feller must always be prepared. Trinidad is a wild town, and a man must protect himself and what he owns."

Professor George Miller studied the store

owner's face to see if he was in earnest. Deciding he was, he finally asked.

"Sir, what do you suggest for protection for a man who never fired a gun before?"

"Well, a shotgun is the easiest to fire and hit something with. But it's hardly practical to carry. There's all kinds of pistols. But you have to practice with 'em. Even with a derringer, unless you're REAL close."

"Well, Sir, I guess I might skip that item of western wear. Besides, I spent enough."

"Professor Miller," said the owner of the store. "Every man out here needs protection. I wouldn't feel right letting you leave my store without it. Let's see," said the merchant, pausing over a glassed-in gun case.

He bent over, selected two pistols, and placed them on the counter.

"Now here's a used .41 derringer and a cartridge conversion .38 revolver. I'll sell 'em to you cheap."

"I don't know how to load these, let alone fire one," said the Professor, feeling some fear at the thought of owning a firearm.

"I have all day. I'll show you the ammunition and how to load both of these. When you have it down, we'll go out back, and you can shoot. I have a little range out there."

To the proprietor's surprise, Miller loaded both weapons and then went out back and shot them. The Professor himself didn't know what to believe, but the store owner had told him he had a natural affinity. He easily hit the targets with both pistols. Consequently, he bought them. The heavy weight of the used pistol strapped on his right hip felt ominous and very deadly. He felt more like a fool than a westerner. When he entered the hotel, the owner saw his change of clothing and that he was armed. This time the man's interest perked up, and he even offered a salute of hello. Amazing what a change in a man's clothing could do. The Professor went up to his room to think.

The exposé that he had once started to write on EUROPEAN LABOR IN COAL MINING CAMPS OF THE WEST had to be thrown out. If he was to return to the university, he must write a paper on some other subject. But what? It occurred to him that he could write a piece on the American Cowboy who actually lived and worked on the ranches. Perhaps he could arrange a visit to a cattle ranch. Would an owner, for a fee, allow him to stay and observe cowboys in action? With this thought in mind, he went back downstairs to inquire. Taking one look at the hostile hotel owner, he decided he would ask someone else. Perhaps he could inquire within the saloon across the street.

It was Saturday, and Baca's Bar was crowded. The big-booted and hatted men were burned deep brown by the heat of the sun. The new garb and white face of the Professor stood out among the weathered men. The Westerners eyed him warily. Either this was a greenhorn, or he had spent some time in the territorial prison. There was no other way a man could look so pale in this country. Being cautious and eyeing the worn holster and used revolver the stranger was wearing, the men in the bar gave vigilant respect.

In the brief pause of recognition of a stranger in their midst, the patrons returned to their pleasures. Men talked and kidded. There were three Mexicans playing guitar and singing. Others played cards at tables, and everyone smoked and talked at once. To be heard, men spoke loudly. The Professor stood for some time, eyeing the crowd. He looked more and more like a tough hombre recently released from prison. Miller was simply deciding where to stand or whether to turn and leave. Several customers exited the saloon. This left room for him to sidle up to the long wooden bar.

"What'll ya have?" shouted the bartender.

"Beer," said the Professor and thought, *When in Rome do as...*

"When did ya git out, stranger?" asked a beefy weathered man in worn soiled clothing.

The man's breath was strong, and his body odor was stronger. The Professor backed away.

"Say," said the man in a fit of anger. "I asked ya a question! Now answer me!"

"Answer what?" replied the Professor in mild caution.

Again the man came close and spoke angrily at the Easterner. Spittle flew as he shouted. His odor was overwhelming, and again George Miller backed up.

"Tough guy? Too good to tell a man the inside dope?"

"No."

"I been there. I see your pale face. Now answer the question!"

"What question?"

"Have it your way, stranger!" said the angry man, and he threw a punch.

The Professor reached for his beer on the bar and turned back. Unaware of the extent of the other man's anger or the punch, the big man's fist missed George Miller's chin and hit his shoulder. This propelled the full glass of beer into the smelly man's face and all down his shirt front. The noise in the bar began to quiet as all eyes turned to the altercation.

"Why you!" gasped the angry, red-faced man.

The odorous westerner wiped the foamy beer from his face and eyes and, in a fury, bellowed loudly and backed away.

"I've killed men for less than that!" he shouted.

Professor George Miller was horrified. He entered the bar less than three minutes ago, and he was already in a fight with a smelly brute.

How could such a thing happen to me? He asked himself.

To Miller's horror, the man was reaching for a pistol at his side. His hand was quickly coming up with the gleaming dark metal in his giant fist. Time seemed to slow, and the reality of the situation startled the educated man's keen mind. In a few more heartbeats, he would be shot and killed. This could not be happening.

With a strange inner quality George Miller did

not know he possessed, he assessed the situation and decided with a deadly calm what he must do to live. He reached for his pistol's grip. He felt it in his hand and jerked it from his holster in a flash of muscular movement. Pulling back the hammer as he learned less than half an hour ago, he brought the barrel to waist level and, without aiming, fired. The big smelly man, his pistol nearly at firing level, jerked back in surprise. A bright red stain formed on the man's shirt, and his eyes went big and round. His face contorted in pain, and then his arm fell, and his pistol blasted into the floor. The big man continued to fall backward, and by the time he hit the floor, his face was already forming into a mask of death.

Time resumed its normal course, and George looked in surprise at the pistol in his hand and at the dead man on the floor. He put the revolver back into his holster and looked up to see faces staring at him. George Miller was amazed at his lack of fear and at his calmness. A man had drawn on him, and he had killed him. He was confronted with a situation that meant life or death, and by his own actions ensured life.

"I seen it, Mister," shouted one man.

Several men repeated the comment.

"Jake drew first!" said several others.

"We're witnesses, Mister," said another. "That's smelly Jake Tanner, and he wasn't never no good."

When the Sheriff came, he found the Professor sitting calmly at a table drinking a beer. George gave his statement, and so did the others in the bar. The Sheriff, who usually asked a gunman to leave, took in the calm demeanor of the shooter and decided for his own health to skip the warning. Before nightfall, the story of the shooting was all over town. Word spread that the light-complected man who claimed to be a professor from back east was probably a hard case recently released from prison.

When Professor George Miller returned to his hotel room, the owner no longer looked on with disdain but hurried over to speak to his latest hotel guest.

"Mister Miller," said the hotel owner. "I was just joking about the price of the room. I'm giving you credit for fifteen dollars. I moved your duds to room number three on the first floor, along with the tin tub."

THE YOUTH, THE CANDY, AND THE STRANGER

"Toby Schmidt, hurry up! I don't have all day to stand here over a few pennies!"

"Mr. Dunbar, you should wait on me like any other customer."

"Now hold on there, lad. You got a real mouth on you. You Schmidts have quite a grocery bill; I have a mind to take your three cents towards what you owe!"

"But that wouldn't be fair," Toby argued. "I earned this money from Mr. Schatzer putting all those bottles in the trash behind his bar."

"Humph! No decent twelve-year-old boy would go near such a place. Ever since your father got killed, you Schmidts sure have fallen low."

"Mr. Dunbar, don't you go talking bad about my pa. He was a good sheriff!"

"Yes, and I'm on the committee that pays the monthly pension to your ma. You just watch what you say, boy!"

"You wouldn't treat us this way if father was alive!

"That's enough! Here! Four jawbreakers, three licorices, and one peppermint stick. Now get out and stop bothering me!"

The merchant thrust the candy in paper, gave top and bottom a twist, and dropped it on the counter. Toby grabbed the bundle and ran out of the store, slamming the screen door behind him. He was so angry that he jumped off the porch onto the dusty street and kept pumping his legs towards the end of town. The boy passed the last buildings and skirted around the open field of weeds and thick scrub trees. Coming to the creek, he found the path and ran with all his might toward the distant grove of cottonwoods that grew nearly a quarter-mile from the village.

That dumb old Mr. Dunbar has no right to talk about my ma and me like that! Thought Toby. *Pa was as good a sheriff as anyone could ever find. It wasn't his fault those bank robbers killed him. Ma said Pa would be spittin' mad if he knew how those 'big shots' are treating us after him dying protecting their money. We deserve a better pension than what they give us. Why, we're the poorest family in town. Everyone looks down on us. Ma says they keep threatening to stop paying. If they do, how are we going to live?*

Toby reached the grove and dropped to the ground, panting. He sat still in the cool shade beneath the wide branches. The boy could smell the green grass and the damp earth around the little stream. This was his favorite spot. A natural rock dam blocked the river and formed a deep clear pool that held the water long enough to quench the thirsty roots of the large silver cottonwoods.

"If only we had money!" complained Toby out loud. "Pa is dead because of them, and this is how they treat us!"

"What's that, boy?" came a raspy voice from behind a large old tree.

Toby, startled, jumped to his feet. He wasn't supposed to speak to strangers, and he had no idea who belonged to that deep voice.

"Who? Where are you, mister?"

"Well, kid, I'm not movin'. You'll have to decide whether to come look or run away. It's up to you."

Toby inched forward and peered around the tree. A man dressed in dark clothing was lying on the grass. He was close to the stream, and part of his shirt was open. A white cloth was tied in a dressing around the man's chest, and there was bright red blood on the bandage. Toby stepped forward.

"You're hurt, Mister," blurted out the youth.

"Yeah, kid," said the stranger. "My horse gave out a while back, and I'm glad I found this here spot. Right nice place to lay and get water."

"Should I run for the doctor, Mister?" asked Toby.

"No, boy. No doctor can fix this here. Suppose though that you fill this canteen and give me a drink?"

The man held up a dark cloth-covered container. Toby stepped forward. Not wanting to get too close, he stretched out an arm and grabbed it from the man. The stranger laughed.

"Kid, I ain't going to hurt you. Sure appreciate you helping me out. What you got wrapped in that paper?"

"My name's Toby," said the boy.

"Glad to meet ya, Toby," responded the man with a groan. "My name's…well, suppose you just call me Slim. So, what you got in that paper?"

"Some candy."

"What kind?"

"Well," said Toby, putting down the candy and kneeling next to the stream with the canteen in his hand. "I got some jawbreakers, licorice, and one peppermint stick. That Mr. Dunbar at the general store sure cheated me. I should have gotten two peppermint sticks!"

The wounded man chuckled and then winced and grabbed at his chest.

"Say, kid, could you hurry up with that water?"

The boy immersed the canteen in the stream and held it down. Water displaced air and the canister bubbled as it began to fill. When half full, the boy pulled up on the strap, and water dripped. He carried it to the man. The stranger reached for it. It slipped through his weak grasp and fell to the ground.

"Kid," gasped the man, now lying flat and out of breath. "Could you give me a hand?"

The boy hesitated, then grabbed the canteen, went to his knees beside the wounded man, and tried to bring the spout to his lips. Water spilled out onto the man's neck and dark shirt.

"Sorry, Mister Slim," blurted out Toby.

The man was too weak to speak. He shook his head in resignation. Toby leaned forward, put one arm around the stranger's neck, and lifted his head. The youth raised the canteen to his lips with his other hand, tilted the container, and let him drink. The stranger took several swallows and gasped. Toby was patient and held the wounded man's head up until he nodded for him to stop.

"Thanks, kid," said the stranger. "I sure needed that. Now, suppose you and I negotiate for that peppermint stick. Been a long time since I et. A very long time since I had me some peppermint."

"Well..." said Toby.

The man chuckled, then winced in pain and lay back flat on the grass. He gasped for air. Toby went and picked up the parcel next to the stream and opened its twisted top. He pulled out the peppermint stick, walked over, and held it to the man.

"Here, Mister," offered the boy. "You sure need it more than me."

Weakly, the man opened his eyes. Toby put the red and white striped stick into his hand. The wounded man raised the candy to his mouth and placed it between large white teeth.

"Thanks, Toby."

A warm wind blew and rustled the shining green leaves. The smooth pool of water made ruffled patterns, and then the gust blew itself out. A western jay called from a distant limb, and two black and white magpies flew overhead and disappeared. The stranger lay flat on the ground and looked up at the limbs above. He sucked on the peppermint, took the stick in one hand, bit off a piece, and began to chew.

"Kid, I forgot just how good this stuff could taste. I'm mighty glad you happened by."

"Mister," said the youth. "How—how did you get hurt?"

"I'm not hurt, Toby; I'm shot. Now suppose you tell me what kind of trouble you're in, boy. I don't have much time, so, if you could be…."

"Ma says I'm not supposed to speak to strangers."

"We're a bit past that, aren't we, Toby?"

"Well…"

"Spit it out, boy. Not much time…."

"My pa was sheriff. Some bank robbers came, and he was killed. Ma, she's worried. Folks are down on us. They promised her a pension, but it's less and less each month, and they're talking about taking it away."

“I see, kid,” said the stranger. “Now, suppose I pay you for that candy?”

“Mister, you don’t have to pay nothing.”

“Oh yes, I do. See, I got another favor to ask.”

“Yes?” said Toby hesitantly.

“When I go. When I stop breathing, you take my saddlebags and run home. You tell your ma what happened here, and you tell her I give you what’s in those bags. For you and for her.”

The man raised his head and arm and pointed to a group of rocks on the other side of the stream.

“You and your ma drag me over there and pile them rocks on me. Don’t tell no one else. Tell her mercy is its own reward.”

With those final words, the stranger lay still, and after a short time, his breathing stopped. Toby stood and stared down at the man. Another warm gust blew, and it rustled the boy’s hair and felt like a warm caress against the lad’s face. Toby picked up his bundle of candy and then went over to the brown saddlebags. He unfastened a buckle and looked inside. The wide opening revealed a pile of bright yellow coins. Twenty-dollar gold pieces! It took two hands to lift and place the heavy bags and wide leather strap over his shoulders. He heard metal coins clinking together. The bags were both full, and it would be a chore to get them home. This was sure a lot of money.

Toby started to leave, then turned slowly and sat down on a rock. He thought for a long time while staring at the dead stranger and then at the bulging saddlebags.

"Mister Slim," Toby said quietly. "You don't know Ma. She will work herself to the bone before she'll use money she thinks might not be honest. I don't know how you came by all those coins, but it don't seem natural. I'm sorry you died, but I can't tell her about you. And Pa, well—he was honest, too. Still, he raised me to think for myself and to keep secrets when it wasn't anyone else's business. I have to hide your saddlebags, and I know just the place."

Toby stood up and went to the dead man. With some difficulty, he dragged the stranger across the creek, dug out a narrow trench, and covered him with rocks. Then he spoke a few words he remembered the preacher saying over his pa. He had fulfilled the stranger's request.

The warm breeze stirred again, and the cottonwood leaves made soft whispering sounds.

The young man could hear his father's voice saying what he had said so many times before. *Son, don't you forget, the man of the family must sometimes make hard decisions—choices that only he can make.*

Toby picked up the saddlebags and headed towards his hiding place. He knew he must make clever decisions on how to spend it. Time and careful thinking would reveal a way. Despite the heavy weight across his shoulders, the youth walked with a lighter step, the worried expression on his face now gone.

BAD CHARLIE SMITH

Charlie Smith couldn't tell the truth if he was hogtied and hanging by a thin rope over a five- thousand-foot cliff. Given a choice between telling the truth and telling a lie, Charlie went with a lie every time. If he couldn't make up something when he spoke, then he wouldn't speak until he could. There were bad men and liars in the West, and not one could match the lies and the twisted actions of Charlie Smith. The name itself was a fabrication, and everyone knew it, but not one living outlaw knew Charlie's real name, where he was born, where he was raised, or his past. Only Charlie knew why Charlie, at age 33, was being such a bad hombre.

Not one thing could crack the hard granite-like facade of Charlie. Even his partners in crime gave the outlaw a wide berth. No one tangled with him, and they talked real gentle and respectful around him, for clearly, he didn't care whether he lived or died. He wasn't afraid of nothin'. This was shown time and again, and there was a chain of dead men along the wild trails to prove this. One thing Charlie could do better than shoot off his mouth was shoot his guns. He was one of the real bad men.

That's why it came as such a shock to the gang at Robbers' Roost when eleven of the outlaws came back with Fletcher's daughter, hands tied behind her back, wearing her Sunday dress and still riding in her father's fancy buggy. Never before had the gunfighter Smith intruded in the schemes of the thieves. Those of Robbers' Roost noted his interest the minute he came to observe the girl, which made the eleven kidnappers nervous. Charlie stared from the dark shadow of a store building's door frame. He saw her sitting in the buggy in the sun's full light. She sat up straight, defiant, and her face glowed with vitality. In her long flowing dress, she appeared willowy thin with the contours of a full-grown woman but also with an athletic fitness coming from hours in a saddle. There were freckles on the young woman's sun-browned face, and she looked squarely up at her captors through blue eyes. Charlie thought they looked the color of the cloudless Utah sky. Her flowing red hair gleamed in the bright sunlight.

Staring at the girl, a change came to Charlie Smith. Instant and conflicting thoughts and feelings ran rapidly through his head. Unusual thoughts came to him he had never experienced before. Her very physical presence made an impact on him. Perhaps her handsome looks prompted him to think the thoughts he had. But he also knew her innocent, and brave demeanor affected him as well. His immediate inclination was an impassioned desire to protect and save her from the demeaning hands of these cutthroats. He had always disliked the one glaring reality of the world he lived in. He hated the company he had to keep. It meant he had only this riff-raff as associates. How he despised their bad manners, their illiterate and desperate behavior. Now he could do something about it. At least for a very short time, he would pick the better company of the girl. Tossing aside his past carefree ways, Charlie made his decision and stepped out and off the store's porch.

Taking one long look at the female captive, Charlie drew both his guns and forced the captors to untie her hands. Minutes before, he had lived and fought beside these men; now, he made the conscious decision to turn against them. For the first time in his life, he considered another human being, and he turned deadly and serious.

"Drop your guns, boys," said Charlie. "Now!"

"What's the matter, Charlie?" asked another outlaw leader with the same last name of Smith. "You want the ransom money for yourself?"

"There isn't much I wouldn't do except harm helpless critters and women," answered the gunman. "And kidnapping and molesting a woman is off my list."

"Are you going against us?"

"That I am."

"You won't get away with it, Charlie. Not against all of us."

"We'll see. Couldn't live with myself if I didn't try. Annie Fletcher, you grab that horse on the hitching rack and get aboard; I'm taking you home."

Despite her attire, Annie did as she was told. She found the stirrup with her left foot and mounted, holding up the folds of her long dark dress as she did so. Bad Charlie Smith pointed his pearl-handled six-shooters. The barrels of the guns followed the track of his steely eyes. With fingers on the triggers, he held the outlaws back as they stared into the twin barrels of the double dark bores.

"Now hold on, Miss Annie," called Charlie. "We got some hard riding to do."

They rode recklessly across the open valley surrounded by mountains and towards the secret, narrow, and guarded exit of Robbers' Roost. It was a cleft in the rock created over the centuries by some giant fault that was opened further by a river and rushing rainwater. As they came to the narrow pathway, Annie Fletcher spoke.

"I know who you are, Charlie Smith. Why should I trust and go with you?"

"Your hands are untied, and you are on a horse, aren't you? As long as I am alive, I'll do everything in my power to get you home safe."

"But why?"

"Like I said, I can't abide a woman being harmed."

"I thought you couldn't be trusted about anything."

"Yeah, that's the way it's been all my life, but with you getting kidnapped, there was no room to be my old self. Like I said, when it comes to critters and kidnapping women I…."

Just then, there was a shot from high up, and

one of the guard's bullets struck Charlie Smith in the right shoulder and knocked him from his horse. Lying on the ground near a large boulder the size of a cabin, he began to feel the pain of the blow that struck him from his mount. He watched as the rancher's daughter jumped from her horse. She leaned over him and dragged him and the horses further behind the huge rock. Instantly, she began tearing long white strips from her petticoat, making pads, and then tightly tying and bandaging the wounds on his shoulder.

"Thank you, ma'am. Now, if you can help me on my horse, we'll try to get you out of here."

"You can't," answered the white-faced young woman as she wiped the crimson from her hands. "They'll kill you."

"We got to try."

There was the sound of pounding hooves. Gritting his teeth, Charlie struggled to his feet and grabbed the rifle from its scabbard. Holding the long gun under his wounded shoulder, he aimed and knocked an approaching outlaw off his horse. The kick of the weapon caused excruciating pain. Charlie grimaced, aimed, and fired again. The bullet thumped into the flesh of a horse. The rider flew high over the head of the dead animal, snapping his neck as he hit the ground. The remainder of the charging kidnappers reined hard and turned away from the deadly rifle fire.

"Feel real bad about that horse. Now, quick," commanded Charlie. "We must get through the pass before they come back."

"We can't; the guards on top will kill you."

"Then you go, and I'll hold them off. The guards won't dare shoot you, or your pa will wipe out the Roost."

"I'm not leaving you behind," said the girl.

"Don't be a fool!"

"Get on your horse. I have an idea."

Charlie stared at the determined face of the rancher's daughter and reluctantly mounted his horse. Annie stepped up on a large rock, hoisted her skirt, and seated herself on the cantle behind Charlie.

"You said the guards wouldn't shoot me, so we'll ride double until we get through the pass."

Charlie grabbed the reins of Annie's horse and tied them to the pommel. He guided both mounts forward, and they passed around the large boulder and into the entrance of the narrow cleft. Charlie held his breath, waiting for a bullet from the guards on top.

"This is not right, ma'am."

"You know my name, Charlie Smith. Use it."

"Miss. Annie, you can't risk your life."

"You did; now it's my turn. Either we get out of here together, or not at all."

"If I had the strength, I wouldn't let you do this."

Charlie was weak and in pain as he hung his head while he urged his horse forward. At times the passage was narrow, and they rode near to one wall, a stirrup scraping against the rock. All along the way, Charlie expected a bullet and worried that it might hit this strong-willed girl. They rode in silence, and Charlie sweated with pain. He felt the moisture drip down under his arms and along his back.

"Ma'am, I mean Miss. Annie, you shouldn't ought to be riding with a man like me."

"Why?"

"You said you knew who I was. Then you know why."

"Whatever you were, I don't care. You saved my father from a great ransom and me from even a worse fate. You took a bullet for me and risked your life against all those outlaws. How can I think badly of you, Charlie?"

"We still aren't out of it, Miss. Annie."

"Yes, I know. But so far, we are free and escaping, and I won't give up if you won't."

"No, Miss. Annie. As long as I can breathe, I'll do my best to get you home."

"You're sweating. You must be in great pain."

After a long interval, the two made their way out of the mountain gorge from Robbers' Roost and galloped onto a wide-open plain. Out of rifle range, Annie dismounted and got astride her horse. They looked back in the direction of the mountain. Horses and riders spewed forth from the gorge entrance. The outlaws were a quarter-mile away.

"Will we make it, Charlie?"

"I don't know, Annie, but we can try."

"Maybe father and his men will be looking for me."

"Let's hope so."

Charlie spurred his horse, and the animal went into a gallop. Annie followed close behind. Two dust clouds rose, one from their galloping horses and a larger one from the outlaws in pursuit. There were more than a dozen, and they were slowly gaining. Their horses were laboring, white foam began to form then flecked off the withers and onto the wounded man and the girl.

"Father's ranch is so far away!" called the girl. "I don't see how we can make it!"

"We'll stop at the rocks up ahead. We'll hold them off, give a chance for the horses to rest, and then continue on."

At the rocks, he gave the reins to the girl to hold. Taking his rifle, he climbed. Resting his long-gun on a boulder, Charlie managed to hit a horse. He unloaded the weapon by firing steadily, shooting several more outlaws and, to his great dismay, because of the wound in his shoulder, two more horses. Up on the rocks, he reloaded and kept aiming and firing until his rifle was empty. He caused no further damage but noted the men riding back and out of range.

Charlie took .44-40 rounds from his belt, loaded his Winchester once more, and waited. The outlaws were out on the open plain. There was no cover and no way for them to come forward. When the horses stopped their labored breathing, Charlie climbed down and remounted. In this manner, the girl and her savior managed to make more distance across the prairie and nearer to the Fletcher Ranch.

Charlie and the girl, for the third time, took shelter behind boulders. With his rifle, he kept the outlaws at bay. He was nearly out of bullets. Weak from blood loss and pain, the wounded man didn't know how much further he could ride. Then both heard the sound of pounding hooves. Charlie turned and watched as the girl raised her arms and waved.

"It's Father! You saved us both!"

Fletcher and his cowboys came riding up in a flurry of dust.

"Annie!" he yelled. "Are you all right?"

"Yes, Father, thanks to Charlie Smith. He saved my life."

"Well?" shouted the rancher to his men. "Don't you stop here! Get going and chase those kidnapping hombres down!"

Fletcher dismounted and turned to his daughter. He hugged her furiously.

"Annie, if anything would have happened to you, I would never have forgiven myself."

"I was kidnapped on the way to church, Father. They still have the buggy at Robbers' Roost. It was Charlie Smith who faced down twenty men. He risked his life for me, and they shot him."

"Charlie Smith, I heard of you. They say you're a real bad hombre."

"I reckon some do, but not to my face."

"Well, I don't know what prompted you to save my daughter, but I am eternally grateful, whatever the reason. Shake my hand."

Charlie reached over with his left hand and winced as the big rancher shook it.

"Mount up, and we'll head home. I have my other ranch hands looking for you, Annie. I'll need to call them off. When we get back, I'll send for a doctor."

"No need, sir," said Charlie. "Your daughter bandaged me up. I can be on my way now."

"Nothing doing, Smith. You get a doctor whether you like it or not. You're a wanted man. On my ranch, you'll be under my protection. Nothing too good for the fellow who saved Annie."

Before they reached the ranch, Charlie passed out. When he awoke, the town doctor was standing over him.

"You hard cases are all alike," said the doc. "Would take more than one bullet and a pickaxe to kill someone like you."

"How bad is it, doc?" asked the wounded man.

"You'll live. Your right arm might be sore for a long while. I'll be back tomorrow to change the bandages. If you had lost any more blood, you would have cashed in your chips."

The doctor packed, closed his black bag, and departed. Rancher Fletcher and Annie entered the room.

"Good, you'll recover," said old man Fletcher to the wounded man. "Annie, I would like to talk to this hombre alone for a moment."

"Don't you be too hard on him, Father," said the girl as she closed the door, and then she leaned against it, listening intently.

The outlaw tried to sit up and then winced in pain.

"How do you feel, cowboy?"

"Like a horse kicked me—and won."

"You're in a tight spot, Charlie. The outlaws want you, and so does the law."

Charlie just lay there and said nothing.

"I need you to be upfront with me."

"If I can..."

"It looks to me like you have no place to go."

"When I'm able to ride, I'll leave and change my name. Been done before."

"And go on being an outlaw?" asked Fletcher. "Is that the kind of life you want to lead?"

"Never knew no other. Been on my own for the longest. I had to be tough to make it."

"I like a tough man. Took a strong fellow to save my daughter. It's the outlawing part I don't like."

"Yeah, well?"

"I'm obliged, and I can help you."

"How?"

"The governor is a friend of mine. I already wired him and got a reply."

"And?"

"Charlie, you promise to go straight and take a job on this here ranch, and the governor will pardon you, on my word."

Smith just lay there. The pain of his wounds showed clearly in his eyes as he stared at the rancher.

"You realize the governor has put all this on my back. So, if you give your word, you've got to keep it."

The outlaw looked up at the older man and said nothing.

"Well?" asked Fletcher.

Charlie Smith let out a long slow breath.

"I don't get it. Why would you want an hombre like me around here?"

"I think you've got possibilities."

"I don't see why anyone would trust me. Not with my past. What I did for Annie surprised even me. All I ever expected was a short life and a fast death."

"You give me your word, and I'll give you a chance for a new start," said Fletcher.

"I don't understand your interest in me."

"If I have to explain it to you," growled the rancher, "then you're not as smart as I figured. Annie wants to give you a second chance just as much as I do."

"I guess I understand that. Just don't know if I can do it. What do you expect of me?"

"It starts with you giving your word. No more lying and no more bad stuff—ever."

"You're asking a lot."

"Annie seems to think you can do it. I'm not saying I like it, but for her, I'm giving you this chance."

"She really thinks so?"

"You bet! Contacting the governor was her idea. Gonna join us or not?"

"I might slip up. You'll have to give me some breaks."

"Some, but not too many," replied the rancher.

"I know I wouldn't make a very good cowhand—I hate them critters."

"That's a problem. Then name a job you think you can do around here," said Fletcher.

"If you let me work with the horses and not the cattle, I'll give my hand."

"Deal," said Annie's father.

Behind the door, Annie smiled and sighed in relief as Rancher Fletcher reached across the sick bed and heartily shook the left hand of Charlie Smith, one-time bad man of the West.

THE TIMID MAN

"Mother warned me not to marry you," declared Mrs. Patricia Barnes. "She kept telling me you were too timid to provide the good things in life. Instead, I foolishly ran off with you to that stupid ranch."

Patricia Barnes stood next to her husband on the Wichita, Kansas train platform. Her children, ten-year-old Christopher and four-year-old Dolly Barnes sat on a bench next to the luggage watching their parents argue. Since birth, it was something they were quite used to.

"The ranch is sold," replied Frank Barnes.

"How much?" asked Patricia.

"Six hundred dollars."

"You mean you worked twelve years on that homestead, and all you got was six hundred dollars for the house and land?"

"If you waited a few months, I could have gotten more, but the banker was the only one who had the cash."

"How much are you giving me?" asked Mrs. Barnes.

"Half," replied Frank. "Here's three hundred cash in this envelope."

"Half is not enough, Frank. There's Christopher and Dolly."

"Alright, here's another hundred."

"Still not enough."

"Patricia, you have nearly two years of a man's wages. When you get back east, you're going to have to make do with that."

"I hate you, Frank Barnes. I hate you for promising me riches, and for dragging me out here, and for…."

"That's enough, woman. We've argued every year of our marriage. I worked on that ranch until my fingers bled. If you had given me a few more years, I would have purchased more land and made it pay big, but you…."

"I'm tired of the work and waiting, Frank. I'm taking the children and going home to my parents. They said they would give me the farm to do with as I please. It's worth a lot more than what you've given me."

"You go back to Ohio, Patricia; that's where you belong."

"Pa," said Christopher, who had left the bench to come to stand beside his parents. "I will miss you, Pa."

"And I'll miss you, Chris."

"Maybe you'll come and visit sometime?" asked Chris.

"Christopher!" exclaimed Mrs. Barnes. "I thought I told you to sit on that bench and watch the luggage until the train came."

In the distance, a train whistle blew and echoed across the flat land.

"It's coming now, Ma."

"You sit with your sister and do as you're told!"

The young man looked pleadingly at his father. Frank Barnes smiled stiffly at his son and shrugged his shoulders. Christopher walked reluctantly back to the bench and sat down.

"Maybe one day," said the father turning towards his boy. "Maybe someday, Chris, you'll have the gumption to stand up to your Ma. When that day comes, you come back out here and look me up."

"Frank! Don't you be talking to my son like that!" screamed Mrs. Barnes.

People waiting at the depot turned their heads to the arguing couple. Then the train whistle blew once again, much closer, and they turned their attention back to the approaching engine. The train slowed, then slowly chugged up next to the platform. The engineer released a plume of white steam as the great wheels slid to a screeching halt.

"Christopher, you carry the luggage aboard and then help your sister."

"I haven't said goodbye to my daughter," said Frank, gathering up the four-year-old into his arms and kissing her loudly on the cheek.

"Goodbye, Daddy," said the girl.

"Dolly, you follow your brother onto the train!"

"Yes, mother," replied Dolly.

Despite himself, Frank teared up at the sight of his two children boarding the train.

"Frank, you were always so weak and sentimental," declared Patricia Barnes. "Now, what about the stock? The horses and the cattle, the pigs, and the chickens? How much did you sell them for?"

"They aren't all sold yet, Patricia. They're in the

stockyards, and I'm waiting…."

"You're cheating me, Frank Barnes!"

"Keep your voice down, Patricia. I am not. I gave you an extra hundred, and if the stock goes for what I think, I'll send another hundred to your parent's address."

"You better, Frank."

"When have I never kept my word to you or anyone else, woman?"

"You promised me riches and a good life, and all you showed me was a hardscrabble farm and a lot of work, and I…."

"The train's loaded Patricia, you keep talking, and they'll leave you behind."

At that moment, the train whistle blew, and the conductor yelled, "ALLLLLLL ABOARD!" The slim, attractive woman with a stern face turned from her husband, rushed to the train car, and agilely climbed up.

"I'll mail the divorce papers!" called down Mrs. Barnes.

"No need to shout, Patricia," said Frank, "I hear you."

The angry woman frowned down at her husband and then turned and disappeared through the door into the passenger car. The train started to move, and Chris stuck out his head from an open window.

"Someday, I'll come back, Pa! You watch! Someday I'll…."

The train whistle blew loudly and covered his son's voice. From the platform, Frank Barnes, teary-eyed, watched his son wave and try to shout above the sound of clanking wheels, blowing whistle, and hissing steam. Frank waved back and watched the train slowly gain speed and then disappear around a curve at the end of town. Everything that Barnes had struggled and worked for, including his family, ended at the very moment the train left the platform. Now that it was out of sight, Frank turned around, adjusted his gun belt and pistol, and walked through the depot. His sole possessions were a horse, saddle, saddlebags with a few clothes and gear, and a rifle.

Wanting to open a savings account and deposit the money he carried, the former rancher untied his horse's reins and led the animal down the street towards the bank. As he walked along, he noticed how quiet the town was. There was only one wagon in front of the general store and only one horse in front of the saloon. Leave it to Patricia to pick a weekday to leave town and not have to face a weekend crowd. His wife was always scheming and thinking ahead. Still, after twelve years, it was clear to Frank that she had never really grabbed hold of him with the unreserved passion the way a woman and man should hold each other. It was hard to believe that it took him so long to figure out that she only married him for security and the potential riches he assured her he would eventually gain. If only she would have waited another year or so. Old man Ferguson was getting ready to sell his ranch. With the flowing spring on his place and the intermittent stream, there would have been enough water to irrigate grass and…

Too darn late now, thought Frank. *Now, what the heck am I gonna do?*

As he walked past the alley near the bank, he saw three saddled horses in the narrow space. They looked like long-legged runners and expensive horse flesh. *What were they doing back there instead of at the hitch rack in front of the bank?*

Frank tied his own horse to the rack and headed for the front. The big bank door burst open, and a masked man rushed out, and behind him were two more. All three men with a revolver in their right hands. The first man, his lower face covered with a large kerchief, was shoved awkwardly into Frank by the two bank robbers behind him. Without thinking, Frank pushed back and then reached for his own pistol. The kerchief fell and was somehow snagged in the scuffle. The face of the man before him was revealed. It didn't change much as he wore a heavy dark beard.

"Out of my way, or I'll blast you!" shouted the robber.

Frank easily finished the scuffle by knocking the fellow on the head with the barrel of his pistol. It wasn't a light tap, and the thunk on the skull sounded hollow as the man fell. The other two bank robbers, in their hurry to escape through the door, got tangled up in the falling body. Once again, Frank used his pistol to great effect and clobbered the second man on the head. But the third thief stepped back to the threshold of the door and fired his weapon. It wasn't an aimed shot, and it took a piece of flesh out of the top of Frank's left shoulder. The former rancher twisted sideways from the bullet's force and winced at the excruciating pain. Then Frank steadied, aimed, and shot the third holdup man in the middle of his chest. The masked robber was thrown back inside the main room of the bank and slammed heavily onto the hardwood floor. A bag of money with paper and metal coins fell from the thief's left hand. Gold and silver coins spilled out, upended, and rolled across the floor.

Within seconds, the bank president rushed to Frank Barnes, along with two clerks. They began talking excitedly and thumping the rescuer of the money on the back. Frank was now bleeding heavily, and his shirt was quickly becoming soaked with blood. From outside the bank, the wounded man heard more voices and then the commands of the marshal.

"Disarm those fellers, and carry them down to the jail."

Frank pushed away from the banker and looked down at the man he shot. Frank could see the thief was dead. Unsteadily he turned and, feeling nauseated from the pain of the bullet, walked off the boardwalk and grabbed hold of the hitch rail. His horse nickered, turned its head, and nuzzled his wounded owner. Frank pushed the horse's head away with one hand.

"Can't you men see Frank's wounded?" yelled the lawman."Let's get him to Doc!"

Banker Dobs on one side and Marshal Corning on the other grabbed hold of Frank's arms and helped guide the wounded man across the street and five businesses down to the doctor's office. By the time they arrived, Frank's shirt was soaked with blood, and it was running down front and back and collecting around the belt holding up his pants.

"I thought I heard shootin'," said Doc Allen. "Why the man's bleeding, and neither of you saw fit to staunch the flow? Don't stand there! Bring him in and put him on my operating table!"

The lawman and banker did as they were told. The doc grabbed scissors and quickly began cutting away Frank Barne's shirt. When the injured man realized what was happening, he complained and tried to sit up.

"Doc! Shirts don't grow on trees. I only have three, and that's my best…."

"Lie down, you fool," said Doc Allen. "You want to bleed to death? Now let me swab this off and get a look at that wound."

The doc used forceps and a wad of cotton soaked in alcohol. The stinging liquid on the wound made Frank wince and start to sit up.

"Well, just don't stand there!" shouted Doc Allen

to the two men. "Hold him down!"

The doctor kept swabbing the wound, somewhat indelicately to Frank's taste. Blood continued to ooze from both sides of the wound, and the physician kept at it in an effort to make a clinical diagnosis.

"Ahh, clean as a whistle," said Doc. "Bullet went in one side of the trapezius muscle and out the other. You're a lucky man, Frank. It didn't touch a bone."

"I don't feel so lucky, Doc. It hurts like hades."

"Well, you are lucky," said Doc Allen. "Pending infection, once I sew you up, it ought to heal nicely."

"Can you do something to stop the pain?" said Frank. "I'm beginning to feel a might dizzy."

"You two hold him down," said Doc Allen, pointing with the forceps and bundle of blood-soaked cotton. "This is going to hurt something fierce, Frank."

"Can you give me something, doc?" asked Frank.

"All right, if you're going to complain, I got some laudanum that ought to help, but you won't be walking around when I finish."

Doctor Allen gave his patient a dose of the medicine and went about cleaning the wounds and sewing them shut.

"Leave him there," said Doc Allen. "We'll let him sleep through the night, and in the morning, you can move him to the hotel."

"He sold his place, and his wife just left," said Marshall Corning.

"Well, if that's what it took to get rid of that shrew of a woman, then I says it's a good thing," replied Doc Allen.

"He'll be tight for money," said banker Dobs. "I bought his place, and I bet he gave her all I paid for it. I'm giving him a fifty-dollar reward for getting the money back."

"I bet you purchased his ranch on the cheap, and it seems to me," said the lawman, "fifty dollars is a mighty low sum for the thousands he…."

"All right, all right!" fended Dobs. "I'll give him a hundred-dollar reward. And by the way, didn't you say you were looking for a Deputy Marshall?"

"Sure am, and after this here display, he's got the job. But a hundred dollars for what he did is not enough, Dobs," insisted the Marshall, pointing a finger into the banker's face. "Unless you want us town folks to start a new bank around here, you will let Frank buy back his place on time for what you paid. No interest."

"That isn't fair," yelled Dobs, his face turning a bright red.

"Fair, or not fair," continued the Marshall. "You wouldn't have a bank if it wasn't for that man. You agree, Doc?"

The Doc nodded and smiled.

Dobs grumbled, "I reckon I don't have a choice, do I? Then I am not giving any hundred-dollar reward."

"Tell you what, Dobs," said Doc Allan. "He saved my old-age money too by stopping those robbers. I'll put in a hundred dollars to help him get on his feet. Maybe the town council will agree to give a bit of a 'thank you,' too. He deserves it."

"Still, I hate giving up that homestead, now that I bought it fair and square," mumbled Dobs. "I had my eye on that place for quite a spell."

"And you paid him six-hundred dollars for it. Seems that makes you no better than those masked men who tried to rob the bank," said the Marshall.

"That's a fact," added the Doc. "Why I remember when Frank and that pretty wife of his came to town some ten years or so back," said the Doc. "I gave that young man six months on that broken down piece of land he homesteaded. He fooled us all and turned it into a paying proposition. Old man Ferguson himself told me he was selling his place to him because he admired that feller for his grit."

"I never knew Ferguson to go soft on anything," declared banker Dobs.

"Nope," replied the Doc. "And I never knew YOU to give out a nickel for anyone…."

"All right," interrupted Marshall Corning. "You two are on the town council. Call a meeting. If you approve, I'll hire Frank."

"I got to laugh," said the Doc, looking over at his sleeping patient laid out on the operating table. "His wife would come in for some pain or ailment, and that woman could blister a hide with her words. She complained about Frank nearly every time I saw her. She said he was timid, didn't have no gumption. I never heard a meaner woman or one that was so wrong about her own husband."

"Too bad about his kids," said Dobs. "I saw him say goodbye to them at the train depot this morning. I know he set store by both of them."

"I think it's a fact," replied Marshal Corning. "Frank Barnes married the wrong woman."

At that moment, there came a loud banging on the front door of the office, and then someone entered.

“Back here!” called the Doc.

A young boy came running to the back operating room. This was Johnny, the occasional runner for the telegraph office at the train station. In his hand, he held a piece of paper.

“Got a telegram!” said Johnny, breathlessly, looking around the operating room. His eyes settled on the wounded and sleeping patient and went big and round.

“Who’s it for?” asked Marshall Corning.

“It’s for him,” said the boy, pointing at Frank.

“He’s sleeping,” replied the lawman.

“I ain’t supposed to…” began Johnny, and then he handed over the telegram to the marshal.

The boy just stood there staring at the unconscious man.

“You can leave now,” said Doc Allen.

The boy looked around the operating room once more, noting the medicines, the acrid smell of the room, and the tray of bloody instruments on a nearby shelf. Wide-eyed, the youth shrugged and then hurried out of the room. They heard the door slam.

“I am the law,” said Marshall Corning clearing his throat, tearing open the envelope, and reading the telegram.

“Well, tarnation!” exclaimed the Doc, “what does it say?”

“It’s from his woman, that Patricia,” replied the lawman.

“For God’s sake,” exclaimed banker Dobs, “read it!”

CHRISTOPHER JUMPED TRAIN. STOP. WIRE MY PARENTS WHEN HE ARRIVES. STOP. IF THAT’S HOW HE FEELS. STOP. YOU KEEP HIM. STOP.

There was a loud and abrupt snore from the wounded and sleeping patient. The sharp sound startled the three prominent citizens of the town. When they recovered, the Doc began to laugh, and even banker Dobs chuckled. Then eventually, Marshal Corning, the stern lawman who seldom found anything amusing, joined in.

“Well, now, if he isn’t the lucky one,” said Doc. “He got his place back, got his boy back, and got rid of that awful woman all at the same time. And part of it, for standing up to bank robbers and getting shot.”

A GOOD DAY TO DIE

He rode into our rundown village from out of the desert. He was dirty and dusty as we were. The only difference was the bright new brass shells in his belt loops, the well-oiled pistol resting in its holster, the fast horse and the fancy saddle upon it. We never knew what he was running from, but the Rio Grande ran past our squat adobe huts, and on the other side was Mexico. It was hot and cloudless, a repetitive, dry, dusty day, with a bright blue sky and the unending piercing brightness. The presence of the stranger made a surprising change in our daily struggle.

Rose's Cantina was nothing but an adobe addition to an old hut along the dusty trail. A few straggling buildings lay across and on either side of the hard clay street. All had flat roofs, and the dried adobe brick walls were crumbling and sagging. It wasn't so much a town as a gathering of a few mud huts along the river. There were no more than sixteen families who struggled with the irrigation ditch and with the rows of green plants that grew in the broken stone plots. Except for the bandito raids from across the border, a rider was a rare thing, and we all stopped our work to gaze at the stranger's intrusion. Dust kicked up from under each hoof of the rider's exhausted horse, and when he dismounted in front of Rose's, we watched him tie the reins to the iron ring and go inside.

Rose had been dead for nearly twenty years. It was now our community meeting place, and all of us threw down our tools and rushed to the cantina. For those with money, there was tequila, beans, and frijoles. Perhaps the stranger would throw some dollars our way or tell us what was going on in the outside world. We all spoke Spanish, but we lived on the Yankee side of the border, and we took some pride in this. Perhaps the gringo cowboy would share our excuse for hospitality, food, and music.

I was all of ten years and Manuel, my father, who had a gift of music, had just made a beautiful guitar for me that I was learning to play. Before the stranger could rest his elbows on the long wooden bar, the empty building became crowded with people. The chairs around the tables filled with men of our village, and father and two other musicians played and sang a song in an earnest manner. All of us children crowded around the windows and door frame as the alcade of our village came forward to greet the stranger. The women rushed to prepare food and drink for the gringo, and the unmarried girls stared. All this before the stranger had a chance to speak. We were like a well-oiled machine, ready to drop our labor and rush to greet any potential customer who could contribute to our poor village.

"Señor, as you see, our village greets you," spoke out the alcade to the stranger.

"Looks like you people are worse off than me. Would twenty dollars, gold, get me food, liquor, and a night's sleep without getting my throat cut?"

"Señor, we are not a bad people, just very poor. A paying stranger is something we cannot ignore. Twenty dollars would be most generous."

The alcade translated the gringo's offer, and there was a great shout. This man was no different than a few other gringos I had seen before. He was on the run and was willing to spend his money. The music continued, and the beans, frijoles, and tequila were brought before the armed stranger. Cheap mescal and tequila began to be served to the older men at the tables. The acting mayor himself took two bottles and began to pour drinks into the empty cups. With the music came smiles, and more food began to be prepared and served to all the villagers. Today there would be no more work under the hot sun. There would be a fiesta because a paying stranger had come to town. There was little enough pleasure for our people, and they would take any excuse to celebrate.

Before the sun set, drink took effect on the men of the village. Many were laughing, dancing, and singing to my father's music. I sat in the thick window frame and watched the stranger and noted that from time to time, he too relaxed and smiled. But he did not drink very much of the alcohol. Then from behind, with a pause in the music, I heard splashing in the river and then pounding of horse's hooves. I looked into the dusk and saw five dark riders on large horses come towards the cantina. They were a group of bandits who came to take what they wanted from our village. Tonight, of all nights, they had come to force their will.

I jumped from the window frame into the cantina

and ran up to the stranger. I stood before him and shouted up into his strong face.

"Señor!" I shouted. "Come," I said with my little English.

"What's the trouble, sonny?" asked the gringo.

"Banditos! Bad men, come quick!"

I reached up and grabbed the stranger's sleeve, and he followed me through a little door leading into the attached hut. There was a lit candle in the empty room, and I blew it out. The stranger pulled his sleeve from my grasp and stopped on the other side of the door.

"I will stay here and watch," drawled the casual voice of the stranger. "Thank you, sonny."

I wanted to run, but I was curious, so I stepped back into the dark and watched what would happen next. I, too, could see through large cracks in the door into the crowded cantina. I waited breathlessly, watching the five heavily armed Mexican gunmen enter the crowded room. The music stopped, and there was a sudden silence.

The leader spoke in mocking Spanish to the men of the village, and he was as arrogant and mean as before. This time, he only brought four of his men with him. Before, there were always so many more.

Without fear, the bandit began to shout orders for food and drink.

"You have so much, you fiesta in the middle of the week?" he called in Spanish. "Well then, you will pay more in tribute."

I watched as the alcade came forward to protest, and the leader drew a pistol and shot him down. In shame, I watched my people cringe in fear. Then the bandit laughed and grabbed at Rosita, my mother's sister, very young and pretty. When she fought back, he hit her across the face. She fell against the bar, and there was blood on her face. All five bandits laughed, and one of them drew a pistol, fired it in the air, and called for food and drink.

In shame, I watched as those who could, run from the cantina. Then the doorway darkened, and the gringo stepped forward into the room. I wondered why he did such a foolish thing. Five against one. Didn't he know my people would not help him?

"That will be enough of that," stated the gringo stranger calmly.

Again, there was complete silence in the room, and the five bad men turned to face the cowboy.

"This is no concern of yours," said the leader removing his heavy wide sombrero and putting it up on the bar.

"I make it my business. Where I come from, we don't hit women."

"This is my town, gringo," said the leader and laughed. "Here, I make the rules."

"No longer."

"Then die gringo!" There was a slight motion of the bandit's head.

Those remaining had scattered to the walls of the cantina, and now the four-armed bandits began to draw their pistols. The stranger, with his right arm by his side, crouched and drew, and thumbed the hammer back with his other hand. There were four shots so rapid as to almost sound like one. Only one of the Mexicans was able to draw and fire his pistol, and the bullet struck the ground. All four of the men slumped heavily to the floor in death. Smoke began to fill the room, and I watched as the cruel face of the leader twisted into a grimace, and unlike his men, he was much faster on the draw. He drew and pumped two shots into the gringo before the cowboy could turn. As the gringo slumped, he fired once last time. The bullet struck the leader in the head, and he was dead before he hit the floor.

I rushed into the smoke and silence of the room. There was blood on the gringo's chest, and he was down on one knee as I went to him. I grabbed his shoulders, and he slumped heavily against me. I could not hold him, and we both fell back to the floor. Rosita came to help me out from under the dying stranger, and it was she who rested his head in her lap.

I bent over and asked, "Why did you do this for us, Señor?"

"Seemed like the right thing at the time," he responded and coughed.

"Oh, Señor, you are bleeding very much," lamented Rosita.

The stranger's face was ghostly white; crimson was pumping from a hole near his heart.

"What is your name, boy?" asked the man looking up at me.

"Isadore, Señor. They call me Issy."

"Do me a favor, Issy. Bury me deep, put a marker over me, and if you can bring flowers."

"See, Señor. I will bring flowers, and we will never forget you."

"There's a money belt around my waist. Take it."

Those were his last words. Rosita and I told the rest of the village what he said. We did bury him deep and put a marker over his head. In his belt we found thousands in paper money. With it, we sent for the priest who came to pray at his funeral. The money was enough to buy guns and hire help. When the rest of the bandits came to us, we were ready. This time my people fought, and I was proud. I kept and used the stranger's pistol in the fight. After, we built a church, and a priest came to serve our growing town. In the fenced graveyard behind the church lies the stranger's grave. Flowers grow over it, and it is I who water them. To our people, he is a legend never to be forgotten.

BLACKSMITH
SWEET VIRGINIA

CHARLIE LATTIMORE

Charlie Lattimore wasn't like any cowboy before or after such a breed was invented. There wasn't a more flamboyant and handsome lad in the entire State of Colorado. Born on a hardscrabble ranch, mostly rocks, sparse grass, and intermittent water, it was a place doomed to back-breaking hard work and near failure every moment of the year. Drought came; the grass withered, plants in the vegetable garden dried up, and the steers, milk cow, horses, chickens, and pigs all suffered. When the drought persisted and the well went dry, the animals were sold or slaughtered. All that was left was the dusty cabin and the long unending views of prairie and mountains. Charlie sprang from just such a humble beginning—hard as flint and twice as tough.

In the Oasis Bar, one ne'er-do-well eagerly asked the inevitable question.

"What are you going to do today, Charlie?"

"Kiss the prettiest girl in town?" suggested one of the group of unemployed lads.

"Round up some money and buy breakfast and beer?" a thirsty and hungry youth called out.

"Nope!" said Charlie, the sparkle in his eye growing with obvious thought. "Haven't decided, but it'll be a whopper when I think up something!"

Charlie liked to brag. All young men of the West worth their salt liked to extol on the common and ordinary. Poverty, boredom, and routine were the enemy, and any cowboy worth his salt would find a way to defeat them.

As the group of coarse young fellows occupied the saloon that late Saturday morning, the bartender tried to take their orders. It was a fruitless enterprise since the night before, the young Westerners had emptied their pockets of all coin.

"Well!" said the bartender in a stentorian voice. "Are you going to order or what? This ain't no play house!"

Astonished at the abruptness, the offended group came to their feet as one. The bartender quickly realized he had overstepped the bounds of decorum.

"Now wait a minute, lads!" announced the bartender. "I, I didn't mean it!"

"You can't offend a man's sensibilities and expect to get away with it!" said their leader, Charlie. "Boys! Go cool him off!"

Eight pairs of hands grabbed the saloon keeper, picked him up, and rushed through the bat-wing doors. Soon, the aproned tender of spirits found himself swimming in a water trough two doors down from the saloon.

"Arrrgh!" complained the dripping wet man. "You can't get away with this. I'll never…."

The offended pistol-packing young men turned back towards the man in the water trough in unison. Eyeing their intent, the bartender stopped in midsentence, his mouth wide open. One of the young wags placed a stick in it—sideways. No doubt the small wooden limb left in the dust by some mongrel or child. The man immediately spit out the insulting object.

"Well?" asked the leader of the group.

"Sorry," said the bartender, now sitting upright in the trough. "Suppose I get out of this, and you boys come back when you have some money."

"So!" said Charlie. "We was all right when we had coin and you pocketed it all, but when we don't, you treat us like curs?"

"Well, I reckon I see your side of it," said the

bartender. "Suppose you let me get out of this cold water and back to my job."

The eight young Westerners who stood behind their leader laughing and jeering at the bartender suddenly fell silent. Charlie stopped and looked around. There, on the boardwalk, stood the town marshal, Frank.

"What's going on here?" demanded the stern lawman.

"This bottle wrangler offended us!" spoke up Charlie.

"Charlie," said the lawman. "How many times have I told you boys to go easy. You'll go too far one of these days, and I'll have to use my badge and the law against you."

"We was only funning!" said one of the group.

"Well, have your fun out of town," said the marshal. "And be careful how you do it."

The bartender took the opportunity to remove himself from the trough. Wringing wet, he marched off dejectedly towards the saloon. With each step, water poured off him, and he left wet tracks on the dry dirt of the street. The young men laughed, and even the marshal had to hide a smile.

"Now off with you ruffians!" said Marshal Frank. "And stay out of trouble!"

The group of nine went to their horses along the rails in front of the saloon. Charlie made a flying mount, and some of the group successfully copied him. Others got astride by a quick toe in the stirrup and a leap into the saddle before spurring their horses forward. The marshal watched them disappear down the street and around the last buildings of town in a cloud of dust.

The lawman shook his head. He worried that he would have to contend with that group one day, especially Charlie, who could outride and outshoot any man in the county. That lad was unpredictable, and the marshal shivered. That was one fellow he never wanted to face down. The law officer had watched the boy grow into a young man, and it could go either way. Charlie would someday cither settle down and make a good citizen or a very bad man. The marshal reflected on this while walking back to the jail.

***

It wasn't long after when four young men held up the stagecoach coming into town. The driver told the marshal they were young and inexperienced and full of vinegar. One of the group accidentally discharged his pistol, and the bullet went through the stagecoach. He missed a seated gentleman by a few inches. The lads took a few dollars off the passengers, as the mail pouch was already delivered.

"You got to stop those boys," said the driver. "They've gone too far."

Reluctantly, Marshal Frank got on his horse and rode to the little ranch that Charlie still lived on alone since his parents' passing. His marshal jurisdiction ended at the edge of town, but he also was a deputy sheriff and took care of that part of the county for the elected law officer. Going up to the door, the lawman was surprised to see that a vegetable garden was fenced in and that well-watered plants were growing in neat rows. The cabin looked in order, and a roof of new cedar shakes shone in the sunlight. A milk cow mooed from the barn, and a pile of newly cut grass lay in a mound before it. Near the home was an array of well-watered and colorful flowers. Up on the ridges beyond the place, the marshal saw several steers feeding on new grass—grass that had sprung up from the last rainfall.

It looked to the marshal that Charlie was making a go of the place. That he wasn't just ramrodding around the country. This made his visit all the more unpleasant.

"Marshal Frank," said Charlie, suddenly appearing from around the house. "I heard your hoss, you come to pay me a visit? Light down; I've got some coffee on the stove."

The lawman was relieved that the young rancher was not wearing a pistol, and he did as the young man suggested. He tied his gelding's reins to a rail and climbed up on the porch. There was a table and several chairs, but the marshal didn't sit. The ranch owner came back out with two cups of coffee and placed them both on the table. The young man flashed the visitor a wide smile, and the lawman's heart sank in guilty trepidation. They both sat down.

"So, what's up, Marshal?" asked Charlie.

"Right smart-looking place," said the officer. "Ranch looks good."

"I try, Frank," said Charlie amiably. "Be a sin to let it go to ruin since my folks worked so hard at it. I sunk a well further up near the mountain and struck plenty of water. Soon's I can afford a windmill and the piping, I'll have permanent running water down here on the place. I have hopes it'll make all the difference during the drought."

"Say, that's wonderful. Your Ma and Pa would be proud."

There was an awkward silence. Charlie kept smiling and staring. The marshal began to get nervous, and his complexion paled.

"Mighty fine coffee!" blurted out Frank.

"Now, you didn't come all the way out here to talk to me about my coffee, did you, Marshal? Spit it out."

"It's my duty to talk to you, Son."

"I'm not your son, Frank. But you were good friends with my parents, and you've known me all my life. I reckon you'll be upfront with me. Especially since I didn't do nothing I'm ashamed of. At least nothing I know about."

"The stagecoach was robbed," blurted out the marshal. "Yesterday, four young masked men held up the passengers. They asked for the mail pouch, but it was already delivered."

Charlie rose to his feet, and his eyes narrowed.

"And you think because my pards and I have pulled some hijinks that we did it!"

"Not so fast! I just came out to talk to you about it."

"To accuse me and some of the boys!"

"Well…"

"Marshal Frank, first off, this is out of your jurisdiction. You're not the sheriff."

"I wired the sheriff; maybe you don't know this, but way out here in this part of the county, I'm also acting as his deputy."

"Frank, if you're accusing me without proof, you better reach for iron, for so help me, armed or not, I'll come across this table at you."

"I told you, Charlie! I came to talk to you real polite-like. You know your tom-foolery makes people place blame. Do you know anything about it?"

"I don't, Frank. That's the truth of it. Besides, stupid, I'm not. If I was to rob the stagecoach, I'd do it BEFORE the mail pouch was delivered."

"That's what I figured," sighed Marshall Frank. "Might you make a guess at who it might be? One of 'em set off a pistol. Driver said it was nervous energy, and a passenger almost got a bullet in the head. Put a hole clean through the coach. Best I stop those young fools before this gets real serious."

"Frank, did you come out here to ask me because you thought I did it or because you wanted my help?"

"Well, if I thought you did it, I wouldn't have come alone, and I would have been packing more firearms."

Charlie smiled, put back his head, and laughed.

"Good answer, Frank! No, I don't know who robbed the stagecoach. I don't think it was any of that bunch I know in town. Believe it or not, except for that Friday night and Saturday morning, I've stayed to home and worked hard."

The young rancher picked up his coffee cup and took several swallows.

"Now that I've seen the ranch, I know that, Charlie. But…will you do me a favor? If you get news or hear anything about the robbery, will you come in and tell me about it?"

"Frank, I like to have my fun, but I'm no thief. You tell anyone else who is thinking otherwise, I said so. I won't take kindly to anyone who says different. Remember that. I'm not a snitch either. But I don't want to see folks hurt. If I hear anything, and it don't hurt a friend, I might come in to talk with you about it."

Again, the young rancher picked up his coffee cup and then drank it dry.

"All right, Charlie. But since these were young men and that group you hang with, well…."

"People shouldn't jump to conclusions," said Charlie. "It's not healthy. And they would be wrong. Being young is no crime, and this here's a wide-open country with plenty of strangers passing through."

"I'm glad we had this talk," said the marshal rising to his feet.

The lawman saw Charlie eyeing the coffee. For hospitality's sake, the lawman picked up the cup and drank. Empty, he set it back on the table.

"Good coffee!" repeated the Marshall.

Charlie stood on the wide porch and watched the combined town marshal and deputy sheriff mount his horse and ride away. When the lawman turned and raised his hand and waved, Charlie slowly lifted his right in response.

***

Tongues do wag in a small place. In town and throughout the county, the first name mentioned on everyone's tongue regarding who might have robbed the stagecoach, was Charlie Lattimore. Who else would have the nerve and ability to shoot a hole through a stagecoach and deliberately miss a passenger? Who else had the wild spunk to pull off such a stunt? There hadn't been a stagecoach held up in the county in a long while, and none of the robbers in the past were spirited young men the driver described.

Charlie had already made up his mind that running with that group of lads in town every Friday and Saturday night was unproductive. He had decided that the "whopper" he would pull on them was to find a decent lady to marry and settle down. To make a success of the homestead—to fulfill his parents' dream—show everyone that his family's homestead could be expanded into a going cattle ranch, and paying concern.

How many times had he heard his father say it? "If only we could find permanent water!" Well, Charlie had found it. With a couple more wells at the base of the mountain and piped down to the ranch, he could irrigate the fields for hay, build a pond, water the steers and barn animals, and grow a lush garden year-round. Never again would a drought ruin the going ranch.

Now that Charlie had matured and adopted his parents' dream, he had to go and be accused of the stagecoach robbery just because he sowed a few oats and was known as a wild cowboy. Why should he be blamed when he did nothing? Just because he could ride and shoot better than the rest of them---or was it because he was poor and came from humble beginnings? It was unfair and unjust. His parents' name deserved respect. Just because his Dad came from Ireland, homesteaded a ranch, and struggled, didn't mean he should be looked down on.

***

Like he had every Friday since he was a kid, Charlie mounted his horse in the late afternoon and headed his mustang in the direction of the Sawyer Ranch. In his saddlebags, on one side, poked out the heads of colorful flowers picked from his mother's flower garden.

Sally was where she always was at this time of the evening, at her parent's gravestone. Her mother had suffered a failing illness, withered away before the girl's eyes, and died. Charlie had seen it. Unknown to anyone, he even found, paid for, and brought in a doctor from back east. "It's the cancer," said the physician. The family thought the doc had come on a friendly visit.

The silver cottonwoods provided shade and a coolness over the rich green grass of the fenced graveyard. The grass was cut, and flowers grew in a perfect square, evidence of the care and respect Sally and her father gave to this place. Charlie dismounted and brought the handful of flowers.

The bouquet was drooping now in the dry air and needed water. Perhaps it was the thought that counted. Sally took the flowers and gave an equally drooping smile. She had been on her knees, but now she came to her feet and faced the tall slim rider.

"Well?" asked Sally. "Did you do it?"

"Of course not, and you should know better than to ask."

"I didn't think so," said Sally. "I know you have been working hard on the ranch. You would have no time or inclination for such foolishness. But in the past…that's what has everyone's tongues wagging."

"It's not fair, Sally, and you know it."

"Still, people are talking, and they're blaming you. There was a second robbery, and it's getting worse. Father has talked about it. He hasn't said it outright, but he's hinted that I shouldn't see you anymore. He's always said you were too wild, that you'd never settle down."

"Well, he's wrong. If he doesn't believe it, tell him to ride over and look at the work I've done on the place."

"I know, Charlie. It isn't fair. But that's how people are once you've made a reputation for yourself. It's a small town, and all those things you did in the past, they're not forgotten. There are a lot of people against you."

"I was a kid. That shooting, riding, and all those wild pranks at the Saturday night dances and around town was just showing off."

"But you scared folks, Charlie," said Sally. "You've won all the shooting contests, and you deliberately hung with that group of shiftless cowboys. Folks have already made up their minds that it was you and some of those lads."

"Well…it wasn't us!"

"Sally!" came her father's voice from the ranch house. "Sally!"

Mr. Sawyer came off the porch and walked towards them. Charlie went out through the graveyard gate and towards the girl's father. If he was going to be told something, he wanted to face it head-on.

"Hello, Charlie," said the rancher.

The older man had a frown on his face, and he did not offer to shake hands.

"Hello, Mr. Sawyer."

"Have you heard?" asked the elder.

"Yes, Sir. Folks are saying I had something to do

with the robberies. It's not true. I've been to home, working on the ranch; if you don't believe it, come and look for yourself…."

"Charlie, it's not that. But it's what you've done in the past and what people think of you now. I've got to ask you to stay away for Sally's sake. At least until this clears up."

"No, Sir, I can't do that?"

"What?" asked the startled rancher.

"I love Sally. Someday soon, I'm going to ask your permission for her hand."

"I won't give it!"

"I'm not the same person I was, Mr. Sawyer. I've made up my mind to settle down and make a go of my parents' place. I've just located a permanent water source, and in five years, my ranch will be one of the biggest around here. You just wait and see."

"I'm sorry, Charlie, but your past behavior doesn't speak well for the future. I'm not asking; I'm telling you. I don't want you coming round here visiting my daughter and dragging her good name down."

"What you say is not fair. Somehow, I'll prove it, but don't ask me not to see Sally."

"Get off my ranch!" shouted the riled father. "Don't you come back neither!"

Angrily the young man mounted his horse.

"You're wrong, Mr. Sawyer!" shouted Charlie and spurred his horse into a gallop.

"Father! How could you?" said Sally.

These were the last words Charlie heard. He was too far away, and the galloping hooves of his mustang covered the angry response from her parent.

***

Word came to Charlie repeatedly from his old friends that he was being accused by his neighbors of the robberies. With a third holdup, more tongues wagged and speculated about him. The young man tried hard to concentrate on the ranch and his work, but his mind kept mulling over what the marshal and his friends told him. It was human nature that he would remain guilty until proven innocent. Something out of the ordinary had to be done to clear his family name. And, it had to be done quickly before everyone in the county set against him. Especially Sally, the one person whose good opinion he most cared about. Anger drove the young rancher to ride into town and tie his reins in front of the marshal's office. He barged in.

"Frank!" said Charlie to the surprised marshal. "Did you hear what folks are saying?"

"Yes. I was afraid it would go this way. So many are talking to me about you. Wondered why I haven't put you under arrest."

"That's the last straw!" exploded Charlie. "Tell me who it is, and I'll…!"

"You can't fight public opinion. Nor fight with everyone who accuses you. That won't help."

"No one has the right to accuse me without proof!"

"Charlie, you examine this by light of day and see it through their eyes. Most of this you brought upon yourself with all those crazy things you and that wild bunch of cowhands have done.

"Last year at the county fair and later at the rodeo, didn't you boys put glue on the viewing benches? And didn't you spike the coffee and punch? Didn't you put burrs under folk's saddles, set off firecrackers, and spook the horses. Didn't you win the rifle contest every year since you were a kid and win the prize turkey and the cash? What didn't you do through the years to rile folks, Charlie?"

"We didn't do all them things you mention," said Charlie.

"That's the point. Folks think you did 'em. Now, when anything bad happens, they blame you and those wild youngsters you hang with, whether you did 'em or not!"

"I reckon I should have eased off some."

"You're darn right you should have. At least let some other folks around here win at a shooting-roping-riding contest without you taking all the blue ribbons and prize money. You live here. You need folks to like you, not find cause to hate you."

"Can't folks see, we was just funning, sowing wild oats?"

"Charlie, you done ten times the havoc, and now you're reaping ten times the grief."

"All right, Frank. But what can I do? I didn't rob those stagecoaches."

"You're a bright lad. Think up something, and do it quick."

Charlie found a tin cup on a shelf. He blew the dust out of it and poured himself a cup of coffee from a pot. The coffee was from that morning, and it was cold. The young man took a sip. Frank watched him tilt the cup up and gulp down the cold coffee. Not once did he grimace or make a complaint. Then the young man collapsed into an extra chair. He tilted it back with a foot and extended his leg, and artfully balanced himself while he commenced to think in complete silence. While ruminating, Frank, the lawman, saw many interesting expressions cross the face of the younger man. The two sat there a long time in silence before Charlie once again opened his mouth.

"Frank," he said. "Make me a deputy. I'll track down those robbers and bring them in."

"What makes you think you can do more than me?"

"You're stuck here with other duties. I can lie along the trail, talk to my friends, and have them look. We can stay at it day and night until we catch 'em."

"It would be a big risk for my job," said the lawman. "Those armed lads and you running across the country will make folks mighty nervous. Someone might get trigger happy and shoot one of you."

"They might do that anyway. The longer those hombres go uncaught, the worse it is for you too, Frank."

"Alright, Charlie, raise your right hand, but I'm asking you not to show a badge unless you have to."

***

While Charlie was organizing his gang of friends to help search for the four who held up the stage, the bank in town was robbed by six young men. A clerk in the bank was killed, and Marshal Frank was shot and wounded. The thieves rode out of town with the people's money, shooting up the place and wounding a child in the process. The marshal was under the doctor's care, and recovery was questionable. Public sentiment went against Charlie and his friends. A posse was formed, and they rode to his place. Not finding him home, they set fire to his cabin and barn.

The young man met and was informed by one of the eight of what occurred.

"If any of you want to back out, now's the time," said Charlie. "The posse finds you with me; they'll make you all guilty. If they come shooting, no matter what, we don't shoot back."

"They might hang us," said one of the group.

"We don't make it worse by fighting back," said their leader.

"Count me out," said another.

"Me too," said several more.

Only three of the group remained by the time the eight young men thought it through, and five went their way.

"Jesse, Ike, Zeke," said Charlie. "I'm mighty grateful."

"Just make sure you show that badge," said Jesse, "if that posse tracks us down."

The four rode in the direction the bank robbers took. They picked up a trail and began to follow it. Charlie was a pretty good tracker, and when horse prints went into rocks, they guessed their way forward.

"Spread out," said Charlie. "When you find sign, make a signal."

They rode in the direction they thought the robbers had taken. It was Charlie who found fresh scrapes of iron-shod hooves on rock. He waved his hat, and the four young men came together and headed towards a canyon in the mountains.

"We'll spook a guard this way," said Charlie. "Suppose we hold up. It's almost night. Let's leave our horses and walk in after dark. We got one chance at this. Let's do it right."

The sun set, and there was still light. They waited another hour. Charlie led the way. Starlight lit the landscape. It was a bright night, and in the open, their forms left long shadows. They came to a narrow cleft in a wall of granite. The opening twisted around to the south and then straight west. At the far end of a cleft of rock, all four saw a silhouette and movement. Someone was standing guard.

Charlie took off his boots and, in stocking feet, made his way forward. One time he stepped on a small cactus. The rocks were also sharp, and he wished he had brought moccasins. There would be time later to pull the spines from his foot. Charlie inched forward, and when he came to the guard, he rose up and thunked him on the head. Together Jesse and Ike gagged and tied the thief while Zeke stood guard. Charlie pulled the spines from his foot and put his boots back on.

There was a wide valley before them. Out on the meadow was a cabin and from its chimney spewed smoke. Cows mooed in the distance, and they saw horses in a corral.

"How do we know for sure it's them?" whispered Zeke.

"We sneak up and give a listen," said Charlie. "I'm willing to bet it is."

"Then there should be five more in the cabin," said Ike.

Crossing the meadow, they came to the shack. A cloth covered a window. They leaned against one wall and listened. A familiar voice was heard.

"Ha! I talked it up real good about Charlie and his pals being responsible for the robberies. They made me part of the posse, and we went direct to Charlie's ranch. I was the one that fired the cabin, and several others set fire to the barn! They'll be busy looking for them instead of us!"

"Why, that's Stewart!" whispered Ike.

"It sure is," Charlie whispered back. "I'm going up on the roof. I'll stuff the chimney. You get 'em when they come out the door."

Again, Charlie took off his boots. He was given a leg up and lay flat along the roof. Crawling upward, the young deputy came to the chimney. He took off his vest and stuffed it into the opening.

"Say!" said someone within. "Something's wrong with the stove. It's…"

There came the sounds of choking and coughing. Then the door opened. Yellow light and smoke spilled out across the yard. First came one westerner, then three others. As each one stepped out of the light, they were quickly grabbed and silenced. Ike, Zeke, and Jesse stood over four of the captured outlaws. The last of the five was Stewart. He saw what was happening and grabbed for a pistol. From the roof, Charlie pointed his revolver at the outlaw and called down.

"Stewart! I got you covered!"

The gang leader turned, saw his adversary, and raised his pistol to shoot. Having no choice, Charlie fired.

***

In the late morning, people came out of shops and stores to stare. A herd of steers was being driven through the town. At the end of the herd, Charlie was seen wearing a shiny badge. In front of him rode five tied outlaws and one dead man. The young deputy stopped at the marshal's office and jailed the robbers while Ike, Zeke, and Jesse herded the cattle to the stock pens.

The doc, the bandaged marshal, and Charlie came out of the jail and onto the street. Doc looked at Stewart sprawled dead across the saddle. There was a growing crowd.

"Well," said Marshal Frank. "I see you brought them in."

"With the help of Ike, Jesse, and Zeke. Couldn't have done it without them."

"Stewart was the leader?" asked the marshal.

"He was the only one of our group who was in on it, Frank," said Charlie. "These other five we don't know."

"What about the money, Charlie?" asked the lawman.

"Every penny of it is in my saddlebags," replied Charlie. "Along with those stolen steers we brought in. Folks can…"

Charlie had to stop talking over the loud voices of the growing crowd. Marshal Frank accepted the money.

***

Charlie, Ike, Zeke, and Jesse were tired and spent the night in the hotel, courtesy of the town. In the morning, word swept through the county of what Charlie and three of his friends had accomplished.

Marshal Frank walked in at the hotel restaurant and joined the four seated at breakfast. When the waiter came, the marshal ordered.

"Just coffee, black," said the lawman, and then he turned his attention to the four young men. "All last night and this morning, folks have been coming in and apologizing."

"Well…they should, after what they done," said Jesse.

"That includes those that were in the posse," said Marshal Frank.

"They shouldn't have burned Charlie's place," said Zeke.

"Heck no," said Ike.

"Marshal," said Charlie. "I guess I'll have to hire on as a hand until I can save up and rebuild. You know what I regret the most?"

"What's that?" asked the lawman.

"Losing that one picture of my folks."

"You won't have to hire out," said Marshal Frank.

"How's that?" asked Charlie.

"Folks around here aren't as bad as you think. When they find out they're in the wrong, they can be mighty forgiving."

"What does that mean, Marshal?" asked Zeke.

"How good are you boys with hammers and saws?"

***

People from town, surrounding ranches, and families Charlie didn't even know came to help with the house and barn raising. Among the many visitors to Charlie's ranch were Sally and Mr. Sawyer, who came hat in hand. Ike, Zeke, Jesse, and Marshal Frank witnessed the exchange. Mr. Sawyer looked embarrassed but stood up and said his piece.

"Charlie," said Mr. Sawyer. "I don't know what to say. I was wrong, and Sally was right. I see the work you done on this place. Sally showed me the well you dug up yonder. Looks like plenty of water. Son, if you was to ask me about my daughter now, I wouldn't say no."

Charlie stared at Mr. Sawyer, and those gathered around waited for him to speak.

"Say something!" complained Sally.

"Well, Sir," said Charlie with a wide grin. "If you put it like that, I'd be plumb glad to take the burden of your daughter off your hands."

BUFFALO BONES

Standing on the porch, Frank Grimes looked over the land one last time. Now it belonged to the bank. He had worked hard all his life, and with one cruel act of nature, the crops failed, and income was gone. With no money, he couldn't buy seed, had no credit at the store, and couldn't pay the mortgage. The farm was lost, a farm he had worked with his father before he passed on. It was hard to walk away from a lifetime of labor and not one penny to show for it.

Sadly, Frank looked again at the fields. He stepped off the porch. A small pack containing everything he owned hung on his shoulders. Now the milk cow, the draft horses, the wagon, and all the tools and farm equipment belonged to the bank. The farmhouse wasn't much. It was sturdy, and the roof didn't leak, but it wouldn't be missed. It was the hundred sixty acres of land, the large barn, the fences marking the boundaries, the sturdy oaks and walnuts he and his father planted that would be hard to leave.

Frank Grimes did not smile or greet the banker. He left the key in the lock of the front door. It was symbolic; it was a key he and his father had never used. Besides, how could you lock up a barn, a farm, the land? All Frank could do was try to close his mind to the hopes, dreams, and memories. The farm had been his life. It was in his blood, and he would never forget it, no matter where he went or how long he lived.

"I'm sorry, Mr. Grimes," said the banker. "Good luck to you, sir."

Frank did not shake the extended hand, nor did he respond. He turned his back on the man and began walking down the shaded lane. He passed under the walnut trees he and his father planted more than twenty years before. Frank walked through the land he so dearly loved for the last time. Turning at the gate onto the road, he started south. He was a grown man of thirty-two with five dollars and change. He didn't even have a horse or a mule to ride. No plan, no destination—the future unknown.

The wind began to blow. It would be a blustery fall and a hard cold winter. There was a natural instinct about the weather in Frank Grimes. The critters started storing early; birds gathered sooner for migration, and fur on the animals was thicker. Those were not good signs.

***

It takes a man a long time to walk from Ohio to the Mississippi. It took Frank Grimes months. He worked his way along, cutting wood, mowing hay, harvesting crops, cleaning out saloons, and performing whatever work he could find. Sometimes it was for food and shelter, and sometimes he got paid. He was a big strapping man, and people liked to hire hard workers. Frank knew how to work. His hands were calloused, and his muscles strong. He wasn't afraid of using his brawn.

On the long walk, he had a lot of time to think. He had been happy on the farm. It was a place of permanence; it was meant to be a place he would live out his entire life. Now, walking along with only a pack on his back, he learned how temporary, how transient everything could be. He was a man alone facing the world.

He had gone to church in Ohio. There were Saturday night dances, church socials, and picnics. He had searched but did not find the right girl. Frank did not socialize well and had a fierce temper when riled. Perhaps that was why he never married.

In St. Louis, there were jobs to be had, but Frank Grimes did not take orders well. While clerking in a general store, he easily handled and filled orders. It was nothing to follow written lists and stack the goods on the loading dock. He even helped customers load their wagons with supplies. But when the owner yelled at him without good cause, Frank rewarded him with a punch in the nose. He fired Frank and refused to pay him. Again Frank hit him. The man ran for the town marshal, and Frank headed west.

He hired on as a stable hand at a ranch far from the city to shovel and clean the stalls and haul away manure. But when the cowboys came to make fun of the new hand, they found the big man did not take to 'funning'. He broke the nose of one tormenter. When his partners came to help, Frank fought four of the riders at once. The ranch owner heard the ruckus and discovered five cowhands with various broken bones. Frank was once again without a job.

"What I need," said Frank out loud. "Is a job where I can work for myself."

A heavily loaded wagon ground its steel wheels over the hard adobe road. As it neared Frank, the wagon slowed and stopped.

"Fer piece to town," said the driver. "Could you afford two bits for the ride in?"

The bearded, dirty man was smoking a pipe, and a white cloud came out of his mouth and curled around his head. Frank noted that the frayed man looked like he could use the money.

"How about ten cents?"

"Done!" The driver smiled a broad grin; a hole appeared, and teeth were missing.

Frank went around the wagon and noted a huge pile of bones on the back. He studied them. They were not cow bones, although they looked similar. The bleached skulls and horns revealed that they were the remains of buffalo. Frank put a foot to a hub, climbed up, and sat in the seat next to the driver. He waited for the man to rein the horses and noticed a right palm turned upwards. Finding his wallet, Frank produced a coin and placed it in the man's hand. Again the whiskers parted, a toothless grin exposed. A thick puff of smoke rose, and the raggedy driver slapped leather.

The old man was burned brown by the sun. The exposed skin on his face and neck was etched with deep wrinkles. His hat was bent, holey, and black with grime. There wasn't one spot on his pants, shirt, or jacket that did not contain a crudely sewed patch.

The bone business, thought Frank, *must not pay well.*

"My name is Frank Grimes," the hitchhiker said.

"Folks call me Smiley," said the old man.

There wasn't much to the driver except patched clothes, skin, and bones. Frank leaned against the back rest. A protruding horn stabbed at him, forcing him to sit up.

"What do you do with all these bones?" asked Frank.

"Sell 'em," said Smiley.

"For what?"

"They'll be ground up for fertilizer," Smiley said, removing his pipe. "I'm told they's rich in phosphorescence or some such thing."

"You mean phosphorous?"

"That's it."

Smiley finished his pipe, tapped the bowl on the

edge of his seat, and hid it away in his frayed jacket.

"Frank," said Smiley, clearing his throat and getting primed. "There's a story to them thar buffalo and to them bones. Now, these here can also be made into bone charcoal. Don't know zackly what that is, but somethin' to do with makin' sugar. Some of these on this here wagon could be made into buttons and used fer knife handles and such."

"I see," said Frank, trying to get comfortable and avoid the sharp horn.

"Now, did you know that fer them Injuns, the buffalo was a regular walking mercantile?"

Frank didn't answer. He was tired.

"Huh?" asked Smiley impatiently.

"No, I didn't," responded Frank.

"Well, they was!" argued the old man.

The heavily loaded wagon creaked along. The rutted road didn't make pulling very easy for the two big draft horses. One of the hubs needed greasing and squeaked with each revolution. Frank finally found a comfortable position, and he began to drift off.

"Now, what do ya suppose them Injuns could get outta a buffalo?"

Again silence.

"Hey! Are you listenin', Mister?"

"Yeah," mumbled Frank. "I'm listening."

"Well, sir, besides food, they used the skins. Can make purty darn near anythin' from the skins. Wigwams, blankets, clothes, shields. Why once I shot an Injun, and you know that buffalo shield durn near stopped a bullet? I had to go and shoot him again."

Frank let out a snore.

"Mister!" hollered Smiley. "If'n youse ridin' in this here wagon, and I's got somthin' important to say, I expect a feller to be po-lite and listen."

Frank sighed and sat up.

"I'm listening."

"Well, them Injuns can make durn near anythin' out of a buffalo. Yes, sir, now that them buffalo are shot off, them Injuns are all gonna starve. T'weren't no calvary that done 'em in. No siree! It was the killin' of them buffalo."

Smiley rested the reins in his lap and grasped his pipe, filled it with tobacco from a leather pouch he produced and lit a lucifer. Smoke billowed, and Smiley smiled and continued talking. Pipe in mouth, reins in hand, the horses pulled and plodded along, and the wheel squeaked.

"Yes, siree!" said Smiley. "Them Injuns can make pots fer cookin' from green hides, use the bones for all kinds of tools. This here tobaccy pouch t'was sewn with an Indian bone needle! They make scrapers, parts of bows, spoons, cups, skull-crushing weapons, sleds, and all sorts of things from them bones. They use bladders to fetch water, hair for ropes, and buffalo chips for fire."

The wagon creaked along, and Smiley kept talking.

"Are you listenin', Mister?" asked Smiley, giving Frank a nudge with a bony elbow.

"Yeah, I am," said Frank.

"Well, I lived with them Plains Injuns. Knew 'em all. The Sioux, the Arapaho, the Cheyenne, thems I liked best. Didn't have no truck with them Kiowas. Commanches, they's the worst. Exceptin', maybe an Apache. Take your hair, every one of them would, if'n they didn't like ya. Was a time I was a strappin' handsome young man, and them Cheyenne took favor with me. Made me blood brother. I used a Hawkins back in them old days and could shoot an ear offin' a rabbit—while runnin'!"

The wagon kept on rolling and creaking, the horses' hooves thudded, the axle screeched, and the trace chains rattled over rough and uneven ground.

"Smiley?" the rider asked. "When is the last time you greased that wheel?"

The old man just looked at Frank, drew on the reins, and stopped the wagon.

"Well now, pardner," said Smiley. "If'n you wants to fix it. The grease is in that there box behind you. And the tools for anything else you got a hankering to fix."

Frank sighed and tried to lift the lid on the toolbox. He had to push some of the heavy bones back that leaned on the top. He finally got it up. Finding what he needed, Frank took the grease and tool for the hub and greased the offending wheel, then wiped his hands in the grass and got aboard. Smiley slapped the reins, and the wagon started. The squeak in the wheel was gone.

"Mighty obliged," said Smiley, and he smiled.

Smiley, just plain talked out, rode on in silence while Frank adjusted his seat and found a spot comfortable enough to let him sleep. Near St. Louis, they came upon a boy with a carpetbag walking along the dirt road. He heard the wagon and horses and stepped off to the side. Old Smiley pulled on the reins and brought the wagon to a stop.

"Hey, boy!" called Smiley. "You be needin' a ride?"

Frank awoke and sat up. The boy held onto his carpetbag like it was the only thing in the world he owned. He appeared to be about ten, and he looked scared.

"Mister," said the lad. "I'm walking to St. Louis."

"What I asked boy is would you be needin' a ride? Won't cost you nothin'."

"Cost me ten cents," mumbled Frank.

"I don't charge young people!" growled Smiley. "What kind of hombre you take me fer?"

The boy came to the front wagon wheel on Frank's side. He handed up his bag. Frank took it and placed it at his feet. The youth climbed up. Frank scooted over, and the boy sat on the wagon seat. He was small and didn't take much room.

"Mighty obliged," said the youngster, showing his manners.

"Boy, what's waitin' in St. Louis?" asked the old man slapping reins, and the wagon moved forward.

"Don't rightly know," said the lad. "I'll be looking for a job."

"How old are you?" asked Smiley.

"I'll be twelve this July."

"What's your name?"

"My folks called me Kit."

"Well, Kit," asked the old man. "Somethin' happen to yer folks?"

"They got sick. Half the town took sick. Even the doc died."

"Cholera?"

"Don't know. Folks just called it the fever. Nearly everybody's gone."

"No one offered to take you in?" asked Smiley. "Relatives or such?"

"Ma and Pa's folks are back east. I was born out here. No kinfolk left after my folks and little sister died."

"Sorry, Son," said Smiley in a uniquely conciliatory tone. "Suppose I told you I know of a place that may take you in, give you schoolin', housin', and feed you for free?"

"What kind of place, Mister?" asked the boy in a trembling voice.

"No need to be skeered," said Smiley. "I know these folks. Good place it is, or I wouldn't tell ya about it."

"Mister, the sheriff wanted me to work for the blacksmith. Said I needed to be 'placed'. I ran away. That Smitty was mean."

"Whoa," said Smiley, pulling on the reins.

He stopped the wagon, bent forward, and looked at the boy.

"Now listen here, lad," said Smiley. "I was raised an orphan back east. It was a bad place, and I ran the first chance I got. I traveled all over this here country. From up in Sioux land down to Texas and I met every kind of folk—some good, some bad. Some people say the Injuns is a bad lot, but I'm here to tell you, people are people, and you got to learn to assay 'em and know which ones you can trust. I know of this here place that will take good care of ya. I know, 'cause from time to time I took interest in how they was treatin' the lads."

"Mister!" said the boy, his eyes widening in alarm. "I'm not going to no orphanage!"

"Boy!" said Smiley. "Listen up. If'n you roam the streets of St. Louis, you'll starve. From starvin' comes stealin'. Them coppers will catch you and toss you in a home for delinquents. And, boy, you don't want to be locked up in one of them places. What I have in mind is a home run by the Sisters of St. Joseph of Carondelet. They'll treat you right; you'll like it."

"You mean nuns? I'm not Catholic, Mister."

"Don't make no mind to them what you are. You think on it awhile."

Smiley started the wagon. Frank eyed the old man with amazement. Not in a hundred years would he have guessed this old-timer was anything but a poor weak-minded fool with a lot of windies to tell. Frank began to make a new assessment of the old man.

The boy was tired. He eventually nodded his head and fell asleep. Frank, too, began to doze off. When he awoke, the lad's head was leaning against his arm. The wagon stopped in front of a building. There was a sign, **St. Joseph's Home for Boys.** Smiley climbed down and signaled to one of the sisters standing on the front step. They talked, but Frank couldn't make out the words. When they finished, the nun hurried away. The boy beside Frank continued to sleep. Within a few minutes, the nun returned with several others.

"Mister Smiley," said the sister in charge. "We are pleased to see you. I am told you have brought us another boy."

It was incongruous to Frank to see the old man be spoken to with such respect. Smiley took gold and silver coins from a money belt under his shirt and placed them in the nun's hand. Frank was shocked. He would have bet his life that this old bone gatherer didn't have a cent to his name.

"I know," Frank heard Smiley say. "You'll take good care of him. He lost his folks, and he's in need."

Each of the nuns shook old Smiley's hand.

"Young man," called one of the sisters, reaching up and patting the youth's arm.

Kit awoke in alarm and clutched his carpetbag.

"No need to be afraid," said the sister. "Welcome to St. Josephs."

Frank watched the nuns coax the boy off the wagon. They spoke gently and guided him up the steps into the building. Smiley looked on and clasped his dry, wrinkly old hands together. When the boy was out of sight, Smiley climbed back up on the wagon.

The old man got the makings, stuffed his pipe, and lit it in a sulfurous stink. Pipe in mouth, he grabbed the reins and slapped them. The horses leaned into their leather collars, and the wagon moved forward.

"Frank," said Smiley. "You mention this to

anyone, and I'll cut out yer gizzard."

They headed to the train yard.

"Now, where was I?" Smiley asked and paused while he looked at his rider. "You listenin', Frank?"

"Yeah."

"Well, about them buffalo. You shoot one for them Injuns in the old days, and they could make a general store out of a carcass. Yes, siree! They could make pipes and fish hooks and what-nots from pert near any part of the animal. Whys, they even made glue from the hoofs. They made all kinds of doodads."

The wheels turned, and Smiley kept on talking.

"Are you still listenin', Frank?"

Frank sighed, gave up relaxing, and sat up straighter. The wagon came to the bone piles alongside the railroad tracks. There were mountains of bleached bones. Frank pulled the wagon up to the scales. After weighing, they emptied the wagon by lifting and tossing bones onto the large mounds. Smiley helped haphazardly and smiled at his helper's strong, easy movements. When the work was completed, Smiley got a piece of paper from the yardman. They drove to the railroad office, and he went inside. When he came out, he had a satisfied grin.

"Frank," he said. "You do good work. You hook up with me, pretend to listen once and a while to my palaverin', and I'll pay ya what you're worth. I'm gettin' too old to do this alone."

"How much?" asked Frank.

"Depends," said Smiley. "But you'll get what's comin' to ya."

Smiley held out a hand. Frank put out his, and a five-dollar gold piece dropped into it.

"I figur'," said Smiley. "There's about forty to sixty million carcass bones out there. It's a cash crop to whoever has gumption to pick 'em up and haul 'em to the railroad, eight to nine dollars a ton further west and here in St. Louis, eighteen dollars. Farmers, ranchers, Injuns, all sorts of folks with a wagon, who got the time, haul in bones. Railroad don't care who it is; they pay the same. You listenin', Frank?"

"Yes, I am."

"Well, I figure it'll take years to gather up all them bones. They're scattered clean from Canada all the way down to Texas. A professor feller I met up with once calculated forty million dollars' worth. That might be stretching it some, but suppose you and me have at it? Work hard, earn money, no one to yell at us or tell us what to do. We got God's own open prairie to look at, and no one place is ever the same. How about it, Frank?"

The old man put out a long skinny arm and a wrinkled brown hand. Frank took it, squeezed just enough, and smiled back at cloudy blue eyes.

Dear Reader,

If you enjoyed reading THREE DAYS UNDER THE SUN (AND OTHER TALES OF THE OLD WEST) please help promote the book by posting a review on Amazon.com and following Charlie Steel on social media.

https://www.facebook.com/CharlieSteelAuthor
https://www.goodreads.com/author/show/3484434.Charlie_Steel

Charlie Steel can also be contacted at charliesteel.usa@gmail.com or by writing to the following address:

Charlie Steel
c/o Condor Publishing, Inc.
PO Box 39
Lincoln, Michigan 48742

Warm greetings,
G. Heath, publisher

www.ingramcontent.com/pod-product-compliance
Lightning Source LLC
Chambersburg PA
CBHW030358310726
48979CB00001B/356

* 9 7 8 1 9 3 1 0 7 9 6 0 0 *